D0435775

AN UNSAFE HAVEN

Also by Nada Awar Jarrar

Somewhere, Home
Dreams of Water
A Good Land

AN UNSAFE
HAVEN

Nada Awar Jarrar

THE BOROUGH PRESS

The Borough Press
An imprint of HarperCollins*Publishers*
1 London Bridge Street
London SE1 9GF

www.harpercollins.co.uk

Published by HarperCollins*Publishers* 2016
1

A catalogue record for this book is available from the British Library

ISBN: 978 0 00 816501 7

Set in Perpetua by Palimpsest Book Production Limited,
Falkirk, Stirlingshire

Printed and bound in Great Britain by
Clays Ltd, St Ives plc

MIX
Paper from
responsible sources
FSC™ C007454

For Bassem,
With all my love.

Chapter 1

They are still on daylight saving and the light, soft and hesitant, comes early, through the gap in the curtains and on to the bed, shaping itself to the contours of their bodies, gently waking her.

Peter does not stir when she sits up. She looks at him, his features in repose beautiful to her, fair skin unblemished, his greying hair fine as silk, an implied calmness to his demeanour even in sleep that still moves her after so many years.

She gets out of bed carefully, puts on her dressing gown and looks back to make sure she has not disturbed him. In the kitchen, Anas is already sitting at the breakfast bar, hair ruffled, his eyes, when he looks up from behind his glasses, uncharacteristically flat.

—Anas, Hannah says quietly. You're up early.

He does not respond.

She places her hand over his and feels a slight tremor in it.

—Is everything all right?

He squeezes his eyes shut and shakes his head. She puts an arm around his shoulder and, feeling him shudder, realizes that he is crying.

—Anas, please tell me what's the matter. You're scaring me.

He finally looks up at her.

—It's Brigitte, he says in a whisper. She's left Damascus and taken the children with her.

She lifts both hands to her mouth.

—I don't understand, she exclaims. Where did they go? What happened?

There is a pause before he can reply.

—I telephoned them several times yesterday but no one was in. I'd been worried since that car bomb exploded in our neighbourhood after I left. I wanted to make sure they were all right, but when I called my mother late last night, thinking they might have gone there, she said they were gone.

—Gone?

A thought occurs to Hannah though she does not say it out loud. Please God they haven't been kidnapped, she thinks. It is not unusual for people to go missing in Syria. Since the revolution and consequent civil war began, there have been tens of thousands of abductions.

—It's not what you think. Anas has read her thoughts.

2

Our neighbour downstairs saw the taxi we always use parked outside for them. They had lots of luggage. When my mother asked the driver later, he said he'd taken them to the airport.

—Thank God. She breathes a sigh of relief. Where do you think they went?

—I'm sure she went to her parents in Berlin. Where else would she go?

—So you're going to call them?

He shakes his head.

—My in-laws moved recently and I don't have their number. I didn't think I'd ever need to get in touch with them without Brigitte there.

—At least you know they're safe, Anas. Hannah is not sure what else she can say in the way of comfort.

—She waited until she knew I'd be coming here for the exhibition and left without saying anything about it. There is bitterness in his reply. She knows I would never have agreed to it.

—Brigitte has talked about leaving before?

He shrugs.

—Since the fighting began, whenever the subject came up. I always told her Damascus is home and I would not abandon it no matter what happened.

He waits for a moment until Hannah begins to feel a hint of his anguish.

—I also said I would never allow the children to leave. I reminded her that they would always be Arab.

3

—But, Anas, you can't be surprised that she would want to get the children out of a country at war? Surely, you can't.

—She doesn't feel the way I do about Syria, he says. Why should she? After all, it's not her country.

Hannah begins to ask him if he really believes any mother, regardless of her nationality, would not choose to remove her children from danger, no matter the cause, but decides to remain silent.

She sits down and feels a now familiar hopelessness rising through her chest, gloom that comes from her many years as a journalist writing about the affairs of a region constantly in turmoil. Silently, she gathers together the thoughts that she will later write down to use in the stories she is always working on.

In the past five years, the Arab world has swelled and raged as dictators have fallen and people in their hundreds of thousands have been killed and millions of others displaced. In Syria and in Iraq, in Egypt and Libya, and in the farther reaches of the Arab Gulf, we have looked on in horror while humanity appears to stumble over itself; and Lebanon, in the wake of all this turmoil, teeters on the brink. There are moments when it seems too big, too unfathomable and overwhelming a reality to take on, when I feel as if I – along with the region I once believed in – am moving through mud, fearful and hesitant, unable to take that next step towards release.

Living in Beirut can be deceptive; it offers a false impression of safety and permanence in the midst of all the upheaval. We feel the direct consequences of the tragic events in Syria, but it is hardly by choice. Is Brigitte wrong in distancing herself from what is going on? And are we, all of us, mistaken in standing by, believing ourselves helpless like this?

There is something else to be learned from the experience of this situation, something to do with the conflict's essential incongruity, even to those of us who are closest to it. Nothing about brutal battles is acceptable, nor are they a normal function of human interaction. This is how people diverge in their perceptions. For the suicide bombers who have been striking in the heart of Beirut or Baghdad, in Benghazi or Sanaa, in heavily populated areas and at times of day when ordinary people are getting on with their lives and the highest number of casualties is likely to occur, for these extremists, there is no such thing as everyday life, nothing in their psyche that points to normality and recognition of the other as legitimate and worthy.

She sighs and places a hand on Anas's arm.

—You're in despair, I know, *habibi*, she says quietly. You have the sensitive soul of the artist that you are and are feeling overwhelmed right now. But things will work themselves out, you'll see. We'll find your family. I know we will.

*

During those foggy moments before complete wakefulness, Peter hears murmurings, imagines himself going outside in search of them, feet bare and his eyes, unbelieving, squinting in the breaking sunlight that bathes the furniture and floors.

It is only Hannah and Anas talking, he realizes.

Getting out of bed slowly, he stands still for a moment and listens further, the voices beyond gently rising and falling. He smiles to himself. It pleases him that his wife and good friend should get on so well.

When he joins the others in the kitchen a short time later, he is already showered and dressed.

—Morning, *hayati*, says Hannah. Sit down and let me pour you some coffee.

Peter looks at Anas but he has a hand over his eyes.

—Is everything all right? Peter asks. Anas, are you OK?

Hannah hands him his coffee and tells him what has happened.

He sits down and waits for his friend to look up. Anas is an extraordinarily handsome man. He has the brooding features characteristic of many Arabs, Peter believes, but in him they are softened by luminous eyes and a palpable quietness of spirit.

—How did she manage to get them out without your permission? Peter eventually asks. Surely they would have stopped her at the airport.

—If anyone did try to stop her, she would've paid

them to keep quiet, Anas says. Anyway, they're not too strict about things like that these days. Lots of people who have foreign passports and can afford it are leaving.

—At least we know they're safe, Hannah interrupts the ensuing silence. Brigitte will get in touch soon, I'm sure.

—Do you have any idea where she might be? Peter persists.

—I'm pretty certain she'll have gone to Germany to her parents. Still, it depends on whether or not she wants me to find her at this point. She's got lots of friends to stay with.

Peter senses hesitation in Anas's voice.

—We can try to find her.

Anas puts his cup down on the bar in front of him.

—I'd rather she got in touch first, he says. I don't want to rush her. She's probably confused and very angry with me right now.

—No matter how she feels, says Peter quietly, they are your children, Anas, and you have a right to know where they are.

A moment later, he wonders if this was the right thing to say to a man in such a vulnerable state. Perhaps empathy, rather than rational thinking, is what he needs right now.

Peter looks at Hannah but her expression tells him nothing. He sighs and lifts his cup to his mouth.

There are times when he harbours doubts about his true nature, wonders whether or not being a physician has made him impervious to the pain of others, or if, even with those to whom he is closest, he has developed a studied indifference, a metaphorical second skin that protects him from the dilemmas of compassion. Some of this disconnection, he knows, he brought with him from America and a childhood home where a show of emotions was discouraged. During periods of clarity, he has seen that, in trying hard over the years to adapt to a culture so different from his own, he has lost the ability to appreciate the subtle ups and downs of human relationships, a shortcoming he is reluctant to acknowledge openly but which nonetheless shapes his everyday dealings with others. Once or twice, when he has tried to approach Hannah with his suspicions, the fear that she might confirm them and judge him further for his apparent indifference has stopped him. At times distrustful of his feelings, he has become adept at avoiding them, working too-long hours to pay proper attention to anything else or simply putting on a façade of detachment that leaves him only in sleep.

As the situation in Lebanon has worsened and Hannah's anxieties continue to increase, he has been close, at times, to admitting a distance even from her, a pulling away from the concentrated passions she harbours, which are a good portion of her essential self. And although he is troubled by Anas's sadness now, he is inclined to leave the dealing with it to Hannah, for whom extreme emotions are an everyday occurrence.

It is often like this, he thinks, my true self appears to me only in bits and pieces, like flashbacks in a film, incoherent but sharp-edged, revealing as much as they manage to hide from me. That surely is why I am bewildered at times like these.

He looks over at his wife again before continuing.

—Look, Anas, I have a friend who is with the International Red Cross here. Maysoun is Iraqi and works mostly with refugees from there, but I'm sure she can find out for us. She told me they have a register of people fleeing war. She'd be able to trace anyone who has left Syria. What do you think?

—I don't suppose it would do any harm to find out, Hannah says, looking at Anas. Let Peter do this and then we can figure out where to go from there.

Anas smiles.

—You are good friends, he says. Once the exhibition opens and I can go back to Damascus, I'll be able to think more clearly and decide what to do . . .

—Wait a minute, Peter interrupts him. You don't have a German passport, do you?

Anas shakes his head.

—I'm pretty sure the embassy in Damascus will have closed down. If you decide you want to go to Germany to find your family, you'll have to get your visa from the embassy here.

—He's right, says Hannah. You can't possibly think of going in and out of Syria just yet. Besides, there have been battles going on very near Damascus the last few days and it's dangerous. Stay on with us for a while longer, until we can work out what to do.

Anas hangs his head. Peter looks on as Hannah puts her arms around him and, for a brief moment, is conscious of the rhythmic beating of his own heart.

When Anas goes inside to get ready to leave for the gallery, Peter turns to Hannah.

—I can't believe Brigitte would leave like that without telling Anas about it, he says.

—Maybe she was worried he'd use the children as an excuse and prevent her from leaving. He could have contacted the authorities and had them stopped at the airport. She wouldn't have been allowed to take the children away without his consent.

—I can understand her wanting to save the children from the war, Hannah. But she should have found a way to let him know she was planning to escape. She could even have come here with the children instead of disappearing like that.

He grabs his jacket and starts for the front door.

—By the way – he turns to ask her – are you visiting another refugee encampment for your articles today?

Hannah shakes her head.

—I can't do any work after what has happened. Anas is absolutely devastated and I need to be with him.

—I realize he's upset. But nothing we do at this point is going to make him feel better.

She looks at him with what seems like reproach.

—He can't be left to deal with this on his own, Peter.

—Anas is going to feel upset no matter what we try to do. He has to cope with the situation in his own way and he's aware we're here to help whenever he needs it.

—Whatever you might think, I will not leave him today. I have to make sure he's OK. Then, frowning, she continues quietly: You know, there are times when we seem so different, you and I.

Before he can be alarmed by what she has said, he decides to make a joke of it.

—Just as well we are and I can help tone down your angst, he says.

But she only turns away.

Chapter 2

From the beautiful residential neighbourhood of Abou Roummaneh in Damascus, Anas drives his children to school every morning, stopping the car to let them safely out, then placing their bags on their backs and watching them walk away, his heart leaving with them, the tug of separation lingering as he drives on to his studio on the outskirts of the city, as he sets to work and anticipates release from the everyday, as he dreams.

With Marwan and Rana, he has tried to cultivate a quietness that had been largely absent in his own child-hood, in which his parents' love had been too intense at times, too enveloping to allow him breath. Growing up, he had had the comfort of knowing that whatever the challenges, whether it was anxiety over schoolwork or rejection by friends, whether he got disapproval from strangers or simply felt disconnected from the world around him, whatever the break these experiences caused inside him, there would always be someone or something to put him together again. His mother making his favourite sweets and the pleasure in her eyes as she watched him eat them; his sisters, both older, helping him with homework, often doing it for him while he went out to play; his father insisting, at the end of the school week, that he walk down with him to the old souk to help with the shopping. Once there, Anas became so engrossed in the surrounding activity and displays, felt so much a part of them, that he forgot his troubles.

Yet he had felt stifled by this closeness at times, and recalled occasional moments of aloneness that stood out as bright and exceptional: the sun on his back as he bent down on the terrace to play, undisturbed, with a new toy, the joy in that anticipation, or at night, a little while before sleep, shutting his bedroom door and sensing in this instantaneous, temporary solitude the opportunity to be utterly himself, feeling the relief in that, the release. He has always understood that it is exactly this ability to disengage, with fluidity and without notice or regret, that makes way for the artist in him, that defines his deepest being.

He remembers the joy his parents had felt when in his final year at school he passed his baccalaureate exams with distinction, the pride and the boasting, their expressions of hope for his future – medicine perhaps, or law, they advised him –and then their disappointment when he had refused, their despair that he would be willing to give up the opportunity to elevate his standing and that of his family in a watchful and highly critical society. But the urge in him to create, to portray in shape and in colour what defined his essential being was too strong to ignore, and for several years, during which Anas and his parents hardly communicated, he had taken on menial jobs that allowed him to pay for occasional art classes and materials, until the day he was able to announce to them that he had won a scholarship to study art in Germany and their resolve was finally broken.

Anas is aware that in defying his parents' plans for him as the only son in a traditional Arab family, he became stronger and more determined to succeed as an artist. But this is not a fight he wants to engage in with his children, not the path towards fulfilment that he wishes for them. He sees instead a flexibility in their outlook that they have gained from their mother; this pleases but also at times frustrates him. It is a mirror he is not always willing to look into.

He works on the top floor of an ageing three-storey building, once the pride of Syrian design, with an open stairwell that looks on to a garden overgrown with plants and a small pond that is long dry; and standing right outside his front door, growing in a huge, ancient pot, is a beautiful jasmine bush that dies gracefully in winter and in spring fills the evenings with its perfume. Inside the spacious, high-ceilinged rooms of the apartment are the light and shadows he has always sought, a weightless glowing, and at its edges, a muted gloom, the suggestion of colour that serves as his inspiration.

He spends the best hours of his day sitting at a wooden table placed directly beneath a large, open window, painting with colours he has painstakingly blended together or sculpting materials which he manipulates with nervous hands, slowly but surely drawing the outlines of his better self, he knows, the man he sees clearly in his mind's eye but who in lesser moments appears dulled and ordinary.

Anas has finally found the recognition that a handful of Syrian and Iraqi artists now enjoy thanks to a greater interest in their work around the world, a recognition that is deserved. However, he comforts himself with the thought that increased material comforts and growing demand for his pieces have neither influenced his outlook nor made him change his work habits. He prides himself on that, trusting that his instincts will continue to carry him through what might turn out to be only a temporary rise. He knows that art is the one thing, above all else, that gives him life.

But if his work has achieved success, his personal life – more specifically his relationship with his wife – has not fared well. That too is a long story which he cannot bring himself to talk about, even to his closest friends.

He had been at art school for almost a year when he met Brigitte at a gathering in the home of a mutual friend. She was tall and attractive, like many of the women he had met since his arrival in Germany, and fair: a striking contrast to his own colouring that appealed to him. Yet he had sensed something about her from the first: a willingness and humility he admired; an interest, too, in him that went beyond that initial attraction. Their affair had been passionate and serious in a way that was unfamiliar to him, demanded from him wisdom that his upbringing and consequent experience had not prepared him for, a view of relationships, of women, that was new and challenging. They had joked once about their closest moments being as lessons in love, with Brigitte as the teacher and he the willing student.

When they married not long after meeting, she had told him she looked on the prospect of moving to Damascus to live and raise a family as a welcome adventure. If she loved her husband so much, she admitted, it was in large part because she was fascinated with his culture, longed to discover a world far outside her own European upbringing.

Syria had lived up to all her expectations at first, as an authentic Arab country that remained largely faithful to its heritage, perhaps – and the irony of this did not escape her – because it had lived so long under dictatorship that Western influences were few and far between. Anas had been charmed, in those first few months after their arrival, by his wife's wonder at the peculiarities of life in Damascus, at its manifestations of old-world sophistication alongside an innocence that he could see moved her greatly.

Once, using a cashpoint at one of the bigger banks in the city, Brigitte had at first been alarmed when a small group of what were clearly labourers came to stand beside her, apparently watching what she was doing. When Anas explained in German that the service was very new to Damascus and that the onlookers were merely curious, she had smiled and gestured to them to come closer and asked Anas to translate as she gently explained exactly how the machine worked. What she had not known, what Anas did not have the heart to tell her at that moment, was that the men were unlikely ever to need the services of an ATM since bank accounts were a privilege that only a wealthy few enjoyed.

She marvelled also at the daily proximity of people one to the other, the houses in the old neighbourhoods attached to one another in rows, their walls porous, voices and emotions filtering through them in the breathing air, people moving through the crowded alley-ways that represented streets, bodies touching as if in a shared dance, the spaces above them filled also with anticipation, and everywhere, at tables eating, in rooms punctuated by conversation, by deathbeds and in silent prayer, the presence of an unseen but nonetheless all-powerful notion of God.

She told him, in those early days when they talked about their almost daily excursions into the heart of the city, that she had never known such clear evidence of vitality, of the feeling that she could, whenever she wished, dip her heart into it and come out overflowing, of the certainty that in loving and being with him, she had finally found her way home.

And if he were to be truthful with himself now, he would have to admit to his wife's influence on his view of their relationship, the honesty with which she insisted they communicate, the transparency in their dealings with each other.

But neither of them had reckoned on the difficulties Brigitte would eventually encounter in trying to fit in with Anas's family. His mother, he knew, had been devastated at the news that he would be returning from five years studying abroad with a foreign wife and did not hesitate to show her disapproval at every opportunity. And while his father and sisters tried to make Brigitte feel at home, there was no question as to their disappointment in his choice.

His family's feelings about his young wife, he was certain, were not personal. Had she been merely a girlfriend who would later return to her own country, they would have found her delightful, would have welcomed her with open arms; but marriage being, to their minds, a lifetime's commitment, they could not see her playing that long-term role with the dedication to social convention that it deserved; worse still, they could not see themselves settling comfortably with the thought of it.

Anas had been confident that once grandchildren came along the conflict would naturally resolve itself, but the birth of his son and daughter served only to complicate matters further. Brigitte mistakenly believed that she and Anas would be exclusively in charge of their children's upbringing; she had not reckoned on the role of the extended family in Arab culture and arguments had ensued between them as a result. It began over little things like the grandparents feeding the children sweets their mother insisted were not good for them, or ignoring her instructions about meal and bedtimes when the children stayed with them, and eventually escalated into a headlong battle over who exactly was in charge.

Disagreements became especially heated over the influence of the family over the boy, Marwan, who was generally considered more important because he would eventually carry the family name.

Anas remembers especially one Sunday lunchtime when, as was their custom, they had all gone to his parents' house. Once lunch was over, Brigitte had asked Marwan and Rana to help with the clearing up but Anas's mother had been horrified when she saw her grandchildren at the kitchen sink washing dishes, had ripped the apron from around Marwan's waist and pushed him away.

Anas had been surprised to find himself taking his mother's side even though he was aware that Brigitte would find this unforgivable.

—How could you let her do that, Anas? Brigitte had begun. Is this how you want our son to be brought up? To think of himself as superior to women and believe they should be relegated to menial tasks?

—That's not what I want at all, Brigitte, and that's not what my mother meant. She's an old woman and she's set in her ways. Why won't you give her the benefit of the doubt?

—Your mother effectively told Marwan he was better than his sister, that it was all right for her to do the dishes but not for him. How do you think that made Rana feel? Are her feelings less important because she's a girl?

—When have I ever acted as if Marwan was more important? You know that's not how I feel, Brigitte, so stop accusing me like this. Haven't you learned anything about our culture in the years you've lived here? Or is it just that you think your Western ways are better?

—Western or not, Brigitte said, what happened was not right and you know it.

She took a deep breath before continuing.

—What's happened to us, Anas? Why don't we talk

like we used to? You've changed so much recently that I feel I can no longer get through to you.

At these words he had been conscious of a resentment towards his wife's foreignness that he feared he might never shake off.

—Do you mean get through to me or get me to think and do what you want? he retorted. You refuse to get on with my family and you are constantly trying to turn my children into something they are not. My children are Arab and this is their culture. When are you going to accept that?

If Anas is not able to ascertain exactly how the trouble between them had started, then he is honest enough to admit to himself that his own behaviour after that Sunday had done little to minimize it. With the growing pressure of work, he began to spend less time at home, travelled a great deal, was secretly relieved at the opportunity to avoid conflict, and left Brigitte to cope on her own. But she had not coped, he realizes now; she had become more isolated than ever, until the day the war in Syria began and all she could talk about was leaving. He had tried to make her see the conflict as he then perceived it: a challenge the country would have to go through before it could move forward, a disintegration that would eventually lead to renewal. Brigitte accused him of naivety, of being unwilling to admit to himself that with the escalation of violence, the conflict was headed towards disaster, had even told him once that he was willing to endanger the lives of his own children to maintain the illusion of Syria as home. His intransigence on that point, his insistence that they remain in Damascus, had driven them even further apart. Other matters came to light for him – and no doubt for her as well – as to the extent of their differences, matters which had not been personal at first but which eventually became so significant that they threatened to compromise their love for each other. It was clear that, faced with difficult circumstances, their backgrounds had led them to contemplate different solutions. For Anas, staying on in Damascus was not only a demonstration of his solidarity for his country but also an act that would serve to reinforce its existence, make it somehow resistant to break-up, while Brigitte maintained that a nation was not defined by its borders but by the unity and common vision of its people.

Thinking of his predicament now, despite the anger and frustration he feels at what Brigitte has done, it is almost impossible for him to imagine a life without her, though he admits to himself that there have been moments when he has hoped for just that, when he has sensed the probable inner peace that different life decisions might have afforded him. Where and at what juncture could I have done things differently? he asks himself.

There is great release for him in art; even now, at the news of his family's departure, his first instinct is to go to the gallery where an exhibition is to be held of his work and spend the day there, among the canvases and away from worry. He is grateful for the support of his friends but for the moment, he knows, there is only one place for him to be.

Chapter 3

Hannah walks with Anas to the gallery in Beirut's downtown where his exhibition will be held. On their way, they stop and sit on a bench on the Corniche, admiring the beauty of the Mediterranean, which, on this cool, sunny day, is smooth and deeply blue.

—I could never live anywhere but by the sea, Hannah says.

—This particular one, you mean?

—Probably, yes. You see how quiet and silky the water is now? Don't be deceived by it, though.

—Huh?

—I mean, Hannah continues, during thunderstorms, the waves are massive. It's impossible to walk here then because you'd be swept out to sea.

—Have you ever imagined living anywhere else besides Beirut? Anas asks after a pause.

—Well, we lived in Cyprus for a while during the war . . .

—Yes, I know. I meant now, when you can make the choice.

She sighs.

—I know many people who have the means and the opportunity are choosing to leave right now, but where would we go? Work is good here and I don't know that we would want to start all over again anywhere else.

—You get satisfaction from your work, Hannah, but the same can't be said for Peter.

—What do you mean?

—We were talking about it only the other day, Anas continues. He's stuck in an administrative job he doesn't enjoy and I think he misses being a doctor.

Hannah turns to him.

—He hasn't said anything like that to me. Surely he would tell me if he really feels like that.

—Maybe he's not sure how to approach it. After all, if he weren't living here, he would be able to practise medicine.

—I didn't ask him to come, Anas, she says impatiently. He wanted to be here.

—He wanted to be with you and you insisted on staying in Beirut.

She shakes her head and looks out over the water again.

—But that's not what I meant to talk about, Anas says. I was asking you if things got worse and some kind of civil war breaks out again, would you be willing to leave Lebanon? It's a possibility, you know, that our conflict will spill over into this country.

—A possibility? A war of attrition is already going on in Tripoli in the north and in the Bekaa, in the towns bordering Syria. It could all spiral out of control, I agree.

But Anas persists.

—You haven't really answered my question, Hannah. What if you had children. Would that make you think differently?

She shrugs.

—I suppose we'd have to think about it seriously then, she replies. I suppose we would be concerned about their safety . . . Then something lights up in her head. Oh, you're asking me if I approve of what Brigitte has done, aren't you?

—Do you think she did the right thing?

Hannah realizes that she's treading on dangerous ground here.

—I don't think she should have made the decision on her own and then left without telling you. But I can perfectly understand her wanting to take the children somewhere safe.

She puts a hand on his arm to reassure him.

He gets up and she follows.

—What if she never gets in touch? he asks her. What will I do then?

—Why would you say that, Anas? What makes you think that? Brigitte wouldn't do anything to deliberately hurt you. I know she wouldn't.

He moves ahead of her and Hannah, trying to catch up, trips and almost falls over.

—Anas, please wait. What's really going on here?

He stops and turns to her.

—The truth is, Hannah, the truth is things haven't been going well between us for some time now. I think she's left me for good.

They fall silent and Hannah wonders, not for the first time, how much longer they will have to endure the repercussions of years of war on their relationships, their family ties.

In 1982, as invading Israeli troops were closing in on Beirut, our family was evacuated on a ship taking Westerners out of Lebanon. My father used his connections with one of the embassies to get my mother, my brother and myself on board the ship. Throughout the journey to the island of Cyprus, the sea surging beneath us, Mother had clung to me and Sammy and cried. I was ten years old and felt a finality in that grief, a suggestion of relief that scared me. How can we possibly leave home? I wondered. Will we ever be able to return, and without Father, are we still a family?

These questions, that initial dread, have never left me.

We spent, along with thousands of Lebanese like ourselves, a number of years on the island, during which we lived in a small apartment near the school that my brother and I attended. I remember that time as an interlude between real life in Lebanon before the war and life there once the conflict ended, mimicking my parents' attitude towards this displacement as a period of anticipation regardless how long or how damaging the waiting to return might be. Whenever there was a temporary lull in the civil war and speculation mounted that the conflict was over, Father would decide we should return home and we would prepare to uproot ourselves, only to be told, days or weeks later, that it may be a little longer before we could pick up from where we had left off what seemed a lifetime ago. Even the friendships that I managed to make during this hiatus had hesitation in them; they predicted their ending even as they began, sacrificing the promise I might have derived from them had they endured. It was not until fifteen years after the conflict in Lebanon began that the warring factions finally signed an agreement that ended the fighting and we were able to return and be a family again.

But coming back had not been as easy as we thought it would be. Beirut had changed almost beyond recognition, not just in terms of the physical destruction everywhere but in the attitude of the people too, those who had stayed behind and harboured resentment against others who were lucky enough to escape the worst of the fighting. The friends I had hoped to meet again had either left for good or were reluctant to renew their relationships with returnees like myself.

When I began attending classes at the American University of Beirut, I felt like an outsider; the bonds I thought I had with my country, its culture and history were tenuous at best, non-existent for the most part. What I remembered of home had been irreparably destroyed by present reality, seemed only to have survived as senti-ment in the minds of exiles. Eventually, my brother Sammy decided he could not live with all these changes and left for America where he studied and eventually settled down with a family of his own.

My career in journalism began soon after I graduated when I went to work for an international news agency, first as a fixer for the foreign journalists who came to Beirut to cover stories on the region, and then as a reporter. It was not long after Mother fell ill and died that I met and married Peter and, in growing older, began to believe I had gained some wisdom.

Since the war in Syria began nearly five years ago, it seems there is no end to the misery it can cause. Those who flee it and seek refuge in Lebanon bring their heartache with them, and for nearly four years now, Beirut's street corners have been manned by insistent beggars by day, and at night, in shop doorways, under bridges, in abandoned buildings and anywhere a nook can be found, there are sleeping figures, whole families, wrapped in whatever they can find to shield their eyes from the light. Many others have fled to Turkey and Jordan, countries that also have borders with Syria. Most recently, hundreds of thousands of refugees have been making the perilous journey to Greece and France, to Croatia, Hungary and Slovenia, and on to Austria and Germany and still further north, in search of safety and welcome.

Things are not as they should be. There is pain where there should be strength, hesitation instead of resolve, and in the places where imagination once had free rein, the Arab people are tied to the foundations of their fears.

By the time they arrive at the gallery, Anas has told Hannah about the problems he and Brigitte have been having and she has voiced the necessary commiserations: I didn't know; I'm so sorry; maybe it's not as bad as you think; and, finally, what can I do to help? She eventually realizes that it is not solutions he is asking for but the simple relief that telling her affords him.

The gallery is smaller than she imagined it would be but there is plenty of light and the carpets and other surfaces are immaculately clean. Some paintings have already been hung while others remain on the floor, propped up against the walls; and sculptures, mostly small to medium-sized pieces, many of which are still swathed in bubble wrap, have been put on stands that are placed at intervals in the centre of the room.

—Do you like it? Anas asks.

—Yes, it's lovely and welcoming.

—That's exactly the feel I wanted for this exhibition. I wanted it to feel intimate.

—Is it OK if I take a look around? she asks.

—Yes, of course. I'll have to get to work on the lighting, anyway.

Hannah watches him walk into the office at one corner of the gallery and turns to explore on her own.

She has always loved Anas's work, the suggestion that it offers more than the eye can see about the circumstances in which it was conceived and executed. The pieces are mostly sombre, the colours he uses muted and unassuming, yet there is something about the square-headed figures he depicts, their limbs out of proportion to their torsos, their features fragmented and eyes usually closed, that moves her. They do not inspire joy, she thinks, but rather compel her to think about the politics of a country that has lived under dictatorship for decades and, in trying to break free, has now lost its way.

She takes a closer look at the pieces within reach and realizes that what fascinates her most in contemplating artistic works is the process itself, the ideas and people that inspire creativity, the phase during which a piece is brought into being by its creator and that moment when the artist instinctively knows that a piece has achieved completeness.

Among these objects of poignant beauty, she also experiences a sense of release, an interval of peace that dispels her misgivings and allows her, momentarily, to dream.

Chapter 4

In the Baghdad of her childhood, in the dazzling summer heat, Maysoun would run out to the back garden, her feet kicking dust in the yellowing grass, and play in the shade of her mother's beloved *naranj* trees, fragrant and laden with fruit. The exact nature of the games she played now eludes her but she recalls their joys with unwavering clarity: the embrace of silence in those seemingly undying hours and a conviction in her young heart that life was unchanging, that love would always be to hand.

She remembers other moments too: her father's voice calling to her to come in out of the sun; the welcome feel of cold water splashing on to her burning face; and, early in the evening, climbing up to the roof with her mother to unfurl the mattresses on which the family would sleep to escape the stifling heat trapped indoors, the marvel of darkness descending, the anticipation.

Later, lying with the dark sky above and familiar, still bodies breathing beside her, Maysoun would listen again for confirmation of that earlier happiness and receive it in the clamouring abundance of stars or in the whispers of neighbours carried across rooftops by the night breeze: memories of Baghdad that would last forever.

An only child, she was born to older parents who had until then settled themselves into the relative comfort of childlessness but who nonetheless welcomed the disruption to their lives that followed her coming. They had loved her with something like indecisiveness at first, but with time and growing confidence in their own roles their affection for her had become more sure so that instead of freeing her as she grew, they tethered her further to the notions of childhood and dependence that she had hoped to leave behind, the idea that in the realization of need is borne the willingness to love and to give.

In adolescence, at a private school for girls, Maysoun discovered the kind of freedom others enjoyed, classmates with European mothers from countries of which she had never heard and which she imagined more exotic than her own – Czechoslovakia and Bulgaria, Norway and Denmark – tall, attractive girls who dressed daringly and expressed contempt for their elders with ease. In admiring and eventually emulating them, she was nonetheless aware of the necessary impermanence of these friendships, for she was conscious of her differentness, of the essential truth that while these young women rebelled with a view to their futures outside Iraq, she would forever remain rooted to the country of her birth and tied to the notion that whatever had come before was preferable to an uncertain present.

The First Gulf War and her father's death soon after she left school brought profound changes to Maysoun's life in Baghdad, bestowing on her the role of her mother's companion and widening her horizons to the many ways in which things could suddenly go wrong, not only for herself but for an entire country and its people. After the allied campaign led to the killing of thousands of retreating Iraqi troops and as many innocent civilians, the crippling effects of international sanctions introduced by the West began to make themselves felt. Maysoun saw herself carried along by a wave of events that she could neither control nor avoid: the first inkling of the harsh lessons that lay ahead. When she thinks now of what was to follow, of her own feeble attempts at struggle against an inexorable deluge, she feels a certain regret; she wishes that things could have turned out differently although she harbours a strong belief that God's will always prevails, that she might have grown stronger for the experience, might have been something other than this undefined, absent self.

She has the colouring of her father's Kurdish ancestry

somewhere in the family's still unknown past, a great-grandfather, perhaps, or one even further back – no one has ever managed to find out. Her fair hair and hazel eyes and skin that is clear and smooth afford her a fragile loveliness uncommon in this part of the world, though it is beauty that with age has softened, become less startling, less of an encumbrance to her daily life. Thinking of her one great love, she is satisfied with the recollection of the myriad ways in which he had looked at her, the wonder and mystery in his eyes and the desire that died with him all those years ago, youth and vision left behind.

In Beirut, getting up and dressing for work in the morning, Maysoun hesitates for a moment before reluctantly opening the bedroom shutters to the noises of the street below. Her second-floor apartment in a popular Ras Beirut neighbourhood makes lasting isolation difficult; it lets in the good and the bad, the brilliant sunlight and the hum of people, the dust and diesel fuel that cause her debilitating allergies, and an inkling that she is part of something animate, breathing, even if she does not wish to be. Sometimes, on the rare occasions when she miraculously wakes to acceptance, the certainty that she is enveloped by God's grace and is worn and defenceless no longer propels her into action.

Since settling here some years ago, she has fashioned for herself an existence that infuses her dreams with calmness but which, in the stark light of day, gives her only reluctant refuge. Often, awakened by the reality of her situation, she cringes at this bustling brawling city and sinks into forgetfulness, imagining the world that might have been, a history uninterrupted by violence and circumstance.

She tells herself that staying on in Baghdad would have been impossible after all that had happened to her there, that despite her attachment to her mother and to memories of home, she had done well to seek a life elsewhere, in a city that, though not ideal, was still in the region and did not have hell and torment in it.

Insidiously, the present always manages to cut short her reveries. In her work in Beirut with refugees from Iraq and now Syria also, in her efforts to survive the ignominy of being and feeling herself displaced, in the relationships she has formed with people, sometimes despite herself, and everywhere her body takes her, through motions and ministrations, the weight of misgivings exhaust her physically as well as in spirit.

And yet, and yet, there are small pleasures that greet her at the beginning of each day. The rhythm of her walk to the office, up a gentle hill and then down again, and the gratifying familiarity of it; the first cup of coffee of the day which she buys from a place near work, milky and sweet just as she's always liked it; the quiet, reciprocated greetings she receives from her colleagues when she arrives at the office; and that moment when, finally sitting at her desk to deal with the tasks at hand one by one, she is aware of a beginning and an end to things and is inordinately comforted by that thought.

Chapter 5

Maysoun is still at work when Peter drops by to see her on his way home.

—I thought I would be too late to catch you, he tells her as they embrace.

—You would have been in another ten minutes. She smiles. It's good to see you, Peter. How are you? How is Hannah? It's been too long since we last saw one another.

—All is well, *alhamdulillah*, he replies. And you?
She smiles.

—I like it when you speak Arabic. It becomes you.

—Even though I've got a long way to go before I begin to speak like a native? He laughs.

—Sit down, Peter. She gestures towards a chair opposite her desk.

—I won't keep you too long. I just wondered if you could do me a favour.

—Yes, of course. Tell me what you need.

Peter had liked Maysoun from their first meeting at a conference on Iraqi refugees who were being processed through Lebanon and on to destinations further away. There was a simplicity, an honesty about her, that immediately attracted him, as did her gentle beauty. He had introduced himself and invited her to dinner at home with Hannah. He had sensed, also, the solitude that surrounded her, though she clearly did not suffer from loneliness, her reserve lending her an air of self-sufficiency that was strangely calming to him. Hannah had also liked her, for the same reasons he had, and it was not long before the friendship was perceived, on both sides, as a particular privilege.

Maysoun's story moved them once they heard it, though after its disclosure and the initial impact it made, it was not referred to among them again. This was less a function of his and Hannah's discretion, than because, Peter thought, Maysoun herself had employed no drama in the telling of it so that the greatest impression left on them was that of deep sadness, of a gradual but inexorable weakening of the threads that hold the self together. When he and Hannah had occasion later to speak about it, it was with the realization that their respect for Maysoun, for her resilience in the face of so many challenges, could only grow with time.

She listens patiently to the details Peter gives her of Anas's story and his concern about the whereabouts of his family before commenting on it.

—Yes, we have the means to trace them, she says. Why don't you tell him to come here to put in an official request whenever he's ready?

—Thanks for that, Maysoun. I'll tell Anas to get in touch with you. But I don't want to keep you here any longer. Shall we walk together?

—Yes, Maysoun says. That would be nice.

In just the past year, Beirut has changed in many ways that are sometimes difficult for him to pinpoint but which once they occur seem immediately familiar. The many beggars in the street who grow increasingly insistent, even at times aggressive; the obvious weariness in people's eyes as they go past; half-empty restaurants; a pall, a greyness that depresses him; a disconnection that instead of feeling like release, brings on disquiet.

He remembers his childhood in Detroit so clearly, he thinks now, because it is a past that contrasts dramatically with his present. He recalls an almost antiseptic quality to those days, an absence of discord and tension that his parents, white, middle-class and liberal, only served to confirm.

Growing older, he had found himself being drawn to the children of immigrants, people whose lives seemed coloured by a chaos and passion unfamiliar to him. Many of his friends were Arab; one in particular became a constant companion, a Lebanese boy whose older sisters were blessed with an exotic beauty that drew Peter even then: the same dark, deep eyes of his future wife, the same impenetrable reserve, hair and skin contrasting like shadow and light, and an almost imperceptible trembling beneath the surface that suggested heightened awareness.

It was not long before mixing, eating and living with families whose lives were prescribed by the customs they had brought with them from far-off places made Peter feel he was acquiring a new identity, one that fell somewhere between bland and overspilling, but which nonetheless did not fit in places. But he only grew more confused about his identity with time; he left school believing he would find it, not in the direction in which his past was bound to lead him, but in the unforeseen future, where experience would lend him the clarity and skill to realize his true self.

At medical school, his days ruled by exams, exhaustion and unrelenting illness, he had finally found the direction he needed, had worked hard to fill the gaps created by a wandering mind, discovered purpose where he had once known only ambiguity.

Perhaps it was inevitable that when he met Hannah while on a visit to Beirut with his Lebanese friend one summer, Peter had been immediately drawn to the unfamiliar in her; sensed also, as they spent more time together, the same inquisitiveness that had propelled him when he was younger, though in Hannah curiosity was hardly a quiet pursuit. Before long, he had recognized an attachment to her that he knew would not fade once he returned to America to complete his studies. There was much at stake for him by then: a job at a prestigious teaching hospital on the East Coast where he would specialize in paediatrics; yet beyond that there was the pull of a woman and her beloved city that would dictate the trajectory of life to come.

When he returned to Beirut two years later, Hannah was waiting as he had known she would be, and since civil marriage is not legal in Lebanon – Hannah and Peter were born into different faiths – they decided to fly to Cyprus and marry there. With time, Peter discovered that while his love for his wife grew steadily, he was less able to articulate it, as though its increasing depth made it more mysterious and inaccessible to him, as though it had expanded to embrace much more than either of them could put into words.

More and more, though, as conflict spreads throughout the region and Lebanon trembles in the midst of it, he senses resistance in himself to the uncertainty of it all, finds it increasingly difficult to separate place from people, to disconnect his love for Hannah from the country to which she belongs.

43

—Perhaps it's me, he finds himself saying out loud.

—Peter?

—I'm just thinking, is it that I'm feeling despair or is it just that I seem to be surrounded by it these days?

Maysoun smiles.

—Probably something of both, she says.

They walk up Sadat Street and turn right in the direction of the sea and towards Maysoun's building.

During Peter's first visit to Beirut, he had enjoyed the quirkiness of the city's byways, the narrow limits of neighbourhoods that, in the minds of locals, were marked and distinctive. Asking for directions elicited conversation rather than providing the information he sought. Often, he would be told to keep walking straight ahead and ask someone at the next corner, or if he were after something in particular to buy, he would be directed to a completely different shop where, he was assured, he could find a better product.

Once, stopping to ask an old man sitting at the entrance to a building where the nearest pharmacy was located, he was surprised by the response.

—Why do you need the pharmacy? the old man asked.

At first, Peter was too astonished to reply.

—I . . . I have a cough and I need to get some medication for it, he said in halting Arabic.

The old man looked up at him with rheumy eyes and made a disapproving sound with his tongue.

—Tsk, tsk, tsk. You young people don't know how to take care of yourselves, do you? Not wearing the right clothes in the cold, going in and out of air-conditioned rooms with hardly anything on. What do you expect? Of course you're going to get sick.

After which, and to Peter's great amusement, the old man grudgingly directed him to a nearby pharmacy as well as advised him what medication he should ask for.

Eventually, Peter became aware of an invisible connectedness between people and places here, a kind of map of everyday relationships, of being, that was easy to follow once you knew how and made for a sense of rootedness which he had not encountered anywhere else.

It seems to him that while in Western societies the inner lives of people tend to shape their existence, the opposite is true in this part of the world where the external is what dominates lives. Perhaps it is a function of the fact that in the West, there is much about one's environment that one can take for granted and, therefore, safely ignore. Peter believes that this is the case only in part, that reality is more complicated, that there is a willingness to concede to fortune in this society that helps people cope: not fatalism exactly but a genuine recognition that acceptance is sometimes the best option in circumstances over which one has no control.

—Sometimes, he says out loud, I think I will never be able to shake off the influences of my background.

Maysoun turns to him and, as she does so, he looks on in fascination as the fading sunlight touches her face, her transparent skin, her eyes, sharp and knowing.

—But why would you want to? she asks. Why would you ever want to let go of the one thing that defines you, Peter?

Chapter 6

Hannah's father lives in the apartment where she and her brother had been brought up, near the sea – though the apartment does not look directly on to it – a neighbourhood which her father says was once the wilderness of Ras Beirut, where jacaranda and lemon trees grew in profusion and, at dusk, the sun swept over vast fields of tall grasses, over the water, in ever-widening arcs of amber reds.

—This, Faisal always tells her in his shaky old voice, was long before you were born, Hannah, when I was a young boy and my brothers and I would come here to play after school despite your grandmother having forbidden it.

She smiles and reaches over to touch his hand.

—Often, we stayed out so late that our father would come looking for us, he continues, calling out to each of us by name in such a beautiful, deep, sing-song voice that we would hide further in the bushes, out of sight, just to listen to it.

—The way you describe it, *Baba*, Hannah tells him, it's not difficult for me to imagine what it was like for you, the joy in that freedom.

Faisal pauses before going on.

—This building is located on the same site where your uncles and I used to play but it was not put up until years later. The moment I saw the foundations being dug, I was determined to live in it, although I was still a student at university at the time and couldn't possibly afford the rent. As soon as I got myself a decent job, I took this apartment and brought your mother here after we were married. Eventually, of course, we were able to buy it and really call it home. He sighs. Life was simpler then, you know. There was more cohesiveness between communities and Beirut seemed much smaller because even when people did not know one another, they were at least familiar with each other's families.

During her almost daily visits to her father, with every telling of these now familiar stories, Hannah finds herself searching for details that she might have previously missed, for the one element that could change her perception of the whole and bring greater clarity with it. What she seeks is not so much to understand the everyday history of this city that came before, but rather to picture it plainly in her mind's eye and so commit herself to its past, to make for herself tangible memories of another Lebanon, a country built on hope and expectations of better times to come, a home that lived in the hearts and minds of its people.

She has some clear memories of life in Beirut as a child, before the outbreak of civil war and the family's consequent escape to Cyprus, memories that are mostly associated with her family, and with her mother especially, young and lovely, her clean scent and dark hair shining. She remembers the way her mother would put out a hand for hers just before they went out, the feel of those soft fingers and, when she looked down, their beautifully manicured nails. As they walked then, Hannah trying desperately to keep up with her mother's long strides, the streets of Beirut seemed to reflect the buoyancy they both felt, the glowing in their hearts.

Once, accompanying her mother on a visit to the home of friends, Hannah had found herself in an enormous living room, the sea – beyond luminous in the sun – framed by the huge window at one end of it. She saw waves that peaked in white and dipped down again into the blue, light bouncing on water and, in the distance, the long line of horizon glimmering, turning pale as it edged towards the sky so that Hannah felt herself lifted into it as she stood, hands leaning against the glass, her tiny body tilting towards the view, melting into it.

There had been family trips to the mountains where

Hannah's aunt Amal and her family spent their summers in a stone house that on one side overlooked terraces of pistachio trees and on the other abutted a hill covered in brambles. Lunch was eaten around a large table placed beneath the shade in the front garden: salads, stews and vegetables stuffed with rice and nuts, and raw meat pounded until tender, wrapped in mountain bread and dipped in seasoning. Afterwards, Hannah and her two cousins – her brother Sammy was an infant still – would tear squares off cardboard boxes they had found in the kitchen and carry them up the hill to a plateau midway on the mountain, high enough that the house looked no bigger than a matchbox but was visible still, and would sit on the cardboard and slide all the way down again, red dirt flying, arms and hearts thrown asunder.

These images, though vivid, are so fragile, so quick now to escape her even as she tries to recall them, that making of them a complete and satisfying picture seems impossible nowadays. In conversation with her father and other elderly relatives, and during moments of solitary contemplation, she fears that Lebanon, tired and faded as it has become, will never again award her that enchantment, that same, untainted delight.

She gets up to greet her father's housekeeper in the kitchen and asks her to make tea before returning to the living room with the pot and placing it on the coffee table. Her father is facing the French doors that lead out to the balcony and she, with her back to the light, looks only at him. Although thin and somewhat shrunken with age, Faisal still, Hannah believes, retains the sense of presence he has always had, with his intelligent eyes and the calmness about him that is evident as soon as one comes near, into a welcoming orbit of tranquillity.

They are silent, enjoying the wet, rippling sounds of tea being poured and sipped, comforting noises that are filled with memories for both of them.

Hannah has always loved the stillness she can share with her father, periods of relief that she did not experience with her mother, who was mostly occupied with verbally identifying things that needed to be done and then doing them with equal vigour. Hannah attributes these gaps in conversation to an older generation of Lebanese, pauses that provide them the opportunity to realign themselves with what is at hand, to assess a situation before acting on it. As a girl she distinctly remembers sitting patiently in rooms filled with people when a sudden quiet would prevail and, to her surprise and discomfort, no one but herself would try to fill it. It is a lesson she identifies with patience and love because neither of these two qualities, she now realizes, can exist without the other.

—Hannah, *hayati* – her father looks searchingly at her – is everything all right?

She is puzzled by his question.

—You seem preoccupied about something, he adds.

—It's the usual worry, I guess. Just concerned about the state of things. Sometimes I think we're never going to know what security is in this country. I'm working on a series of articles for a British newspaper and the more I discover about what's going on in this part of the world, the more despair I feel.

For a long time he does not say anything and she begins to think he might be dropping off in the silence.

—I was seventeen when the war began, Faisal finally says. All hell was breaking loose in Europe, but to us here it seemed a million miles away.

Hannah suddenly realizes that her father is referring to the Second World War.

—Even while millions were dying and the map of the world was being redrawn, he continues, we were lost in our own troubles, trying to fight for this country's freedom from French control. I joined youth groups and went to meetings and took part in demonstrations calling for independence. Some of these activities were punishable by death at the time, you know. People were accused of sedition and hanged for a lot less by the Mandate authorities.

—The martyrs who fought for our independence, Hannah exclaims. We were taught about them at school.

Her father nods and continues.

—It was all such a long time ago that sometimes I have difficulty recalling exactly the feelings associated with it, the uncertainties and the anticipation. But what I cannot forget is the sense of urgency that surrounded those times, an urgency that made us think this period would never come to an end. We were wrong though.

—About the success of the fight?

—Maybe it's just that we got older and too cynical to care, he says.

—Not cynical, she tells him. You were just caught up with the vagaries of everyday life.

During our exile to Cyprus while Lebanon's civil war raged on, Father would come to visit every few weeks, staying just long enough to remind us of himself, so that sometimes it seemed he had been with us only in dreams, so fleeting was his presence, so light the grooves he left on my heart. Although I resented his absence at the time, I later understood that this impression of impermanence had less to do with the time that he spent with us than where he spent it. Father was only half himself when away from Lebanon, not because he had been diminished for want of home but because everything about him that was most true had Lebanon as its anchor.

Hannah wonders for a moment if this is also now true for her, if in leaving Lebanon, she might find it difficult to keep the pieces of herself together. Remaining whole would be impossible. She recalls that when she had first told Faisal of her decision to marry Peter, he asked her if she intended to go to America with him.

—He will remain here to be with us, *Baba*, Hannah had reassured him. We will be his home.

Her father had smiled and said nothing more.

She gets up and stands behind Faisal's chair, bending down to wrap her arms around him. A breeze comes in through the French doors and they smell the sea in it as it blows gently on to their faces.

—Thank you, *Baba*, Hannah whispers into the old man's ears. Thank you, *habibi*.

Chapter 7

On the drive back to Beirut, a few days later, Hannah is aware of almost overwhelming tiredness. She has been to numerous encampments, has spoken to dozens of refugees and noted so many disturbing stories that she is not sure where or how she might begin telling them.

Rifling through her bag, she takes out a thick pile of the small, lined notebooks she uses for interviews and attempts to sort through them. Would arranging them by region be best, she wonders, the regions in Syria from where the refugees have come or the areas of Lebanon where they consequently settled? Should she focus on communities, the number of Shia, Sunni, Christian or Druze who have fled, or is it more important that she keep the most horrifying stories uppermost in her mind, the family members killed in bombings, for example, the homes and communities destroyed, the injuries sustained, the accounts of children traumatized by what they have seen and experienced, the beheadings, beatings and barbarism they witnessed, or the anguish felt by their elders at leaving homes and property behind and the harrowing tales of escape?

At moments like these, she recognizes the advantage photojournalists and television reporters have in covering tragedy; pictures say more than words ever could, their impact is immediate, their portrayal of suffering and urgency unequivocal. She suspects that whatever she eventually writes will not manage to express what she knows is true: the unyielding pull of despair, and, despite the odds, the inexorable reality of expecting something better.

She thinks of their eyes especially, questioning, pleading and trusting eyes; she still feels the small hands of children grasping tightly on to hers; she pictures the recognition on the faces of the women and men she met of a shared humanity, of the potential in meeting like this, in chronicling these extraordinary events.

Of all the images that struck her today, the one she cannot stop thinking about is the clothes line that had hung around the outside of one of the tents in the last encampment, the children's clothes, a neat procession of trousers and shirts, jeans and pyjamas, diminutive and faded, appealing to her in a way she could not explain. Ahead, on either side of the dirt path, stretched two long rows of these makeshift tents, sheets of white tarpaulin with the UNHCR name and logo stamped on to them mounted on to wooden slabs to create a semblance of space, a suggestion of privacy. It would not have occurred to her that the refugees would be so proud of these simple dwellings, the men for having put them up with their own hands, the women for maintaining order in them, but this was exactly what she had sensed as her feet came to an abrupt stop and all she could do was stare at the clothes line in wonder.

The skinny young man with the gelled-back hair who had agreed to show her around the campground when she first arrived stood beside her, quiet though clearly waiting for some sign of willingness on her part to go ahead with the tour. She had felt his presence like a hum on the outlines of her skin, was conscious of his expectation, but still she could not move.

Above, the sky was blue, though she had a momentary impression of it descending gradually towards her in the breeze that touched her hair and blew gestures into the children's garments, trousers lifting forward as if on a swing, a bright pink top simulating a wave with its sleeve.

It astonished her that she could make out too the scenes that had unfolded behind her as she advanced: the tiny mobile clinic where a heavily bearded young doctor treated minor cuts and bruises and dispensed medications to a queue of refugees waiting outside; the movement of people in and out of the encampment with the sound of traffic from a nearby highway electrifying the air; the stench emanating from the filthy, rubbish-filled stream that ran alongside the camp which, according to the doctor, was the principal reason behind the infestation of parasites in the systems of so many of the children in the camp; the glassed-in café where she and the taxi driver had stopped for refreshment midway through their journey, the sweet, tangy taste of homemade lemonade and the little boy, brown and dirty, who had stood begging at the café entrance and smiled when she bought him a sandwich and a drink; the shopkeeper who had directed them to the encampment, muttering under his breath something about the plague of refugees who had descended on the area; the checkpoint they had passed earlier that morning on the road leading down to the eastern Bekaa, where young soldiers, one of whom had a cut on his cheek that oozed a thin trickle of blood down his face, waved them on; the trip from Beirut and she turning back to wave to Peter out of the car window, calling out that she would see him later that evening; and, most of all, the sudden indisputable certainty she had gained that in coming here, in being a part of this, however briefly, she was experiencing intervals of peace.

Leaving the village of Bar Elias behind, we make our way back, Saturday-afternoon traffic leading through the town of Chtoura and on to the capital Beirut heavy and slow. In the back of the taxi, my journalist's paraphernalia is scattered on the seat beside me: pencils and several notepads; copies of UNHCR reports listing refugee numbers, aid disbursement and other statistics; an old map so embarrassingly out of date that it describes Lebanon as a country of merely three million people, the majority of whom being Maronite Christians; and somewhere out of sight, hidden beneath the mess that also includes an empty water bottle and the remains of a packet of biscuits the driver and I shared on our way over this morning, is a disposable camera which I will have developed and give my colleague from England to use for reference when he takes the professional photographs that will accompany this article.

The pictures, I know, will describe events in a way that no words, no matter how eloquent, ever can; will pull at heartstrings without the added encumbrance of intellect and reason. I put my pencil down and stare out at the shifting landscape, feeling remorse for the stories that slip from my fingers every time I attempt to write them down.

Chapter 8

It happens as they make their way back home, discussing the possible outcome of Maysoun's search for Anas's family, wondering what else they can do or say to comfort their friend.

They stop to cross the street at a busy intersection a few minutes away from their building, a traffic light that most drivers and pedestrians tend to ignore, and observe the chaos as drivers manoeuvre their vehicles through narrow gaps in the traffic, past cars that are double-parked on either side and between darting pedestrians. The small shops on either side of the road are also busy, women buying groceries on their return home from work, children running in and out of stationers for school supplies, people waiting to be served outside a sweetshop famous for its *baqlawa* and, on the pavement, constant movement.

Hannah is nervous because a group of refugees

congregated at the intersection, as usual, do not seem wary enough of the cars whizzing past. It is getting dark and the street lights have not come on yet. The refugees are like shadows, she thinks, colourless and in some ways invisible to everyone else. She has seen them here before, remembers especially a young woman with a very young boy sitting together on the median strip running down the centre of the road. When night begins to fall, Hannah has watched the young woman wrap the boy tightly in her arms, both of them sitting very still, the little boy's head on his mother's shoulder, eyes open and searching. It is a disturbing sight.

Tonight, though, the little boy is up and about, moving between vehicles, at times running after them and begging for money. But before Hannah can point this out to Peter, the boy grabs the door handle of a large four-wheel drive and jumps on to the car just as the light changes and the vehicle begins to move forward. He is so small she is almost sure that the driver will not have seen him. The boy's head snaps back and he is thrown off the car and on to the road with a heavy thud. The mother screams and the car immediately behind comes to an abrupt halt. Hannah and Peter run towards the child, gesturing to the vehicles on either side of the road to stop.

The driver of the four-wheel drive walks over to them.

—What happened? he asks anxiously. I swear I didn't see him until it was too late.

People get out of their cars and come up to see what has happened.

Peter bends down to check on the boy as the mother tries to pick her son up, her wailing overwhelming the commotion around them. Hannah holds her back.

—My husband is a doctor, she says in a firm voice. Let him take care of your son.

Someone pulls the woman further away and she stands at a distance, whimpering quietly now.

—What was the child doing in the middle of the road? someone protests.

—They should have a policeman at this junction, another man says. It's getting dangerous.

—It's dangerous because these people insist on accosting us and begging for money.

—Is the child all right? Shouldn't someone take him to hospital?

Hannah squats down beside Peter and watches him check the child's pulse and gently pull up one of his eyelids. The little boy begins to stir.

Moments later, Peter turns to Hannah.

—I think he's going to be OK. But it would be a good idea to take him to A & E to be properly checked. He has to be kept awake for a while to make sure he's not concussed and that the shock hasn't been too much for him.

He lifts the child off the ground and feels the back of his head.

—Nothing seems to be broken, he says, urging the boy to stand up on his own.

A man comes out of one of the shops on the corner with two bottles of water for the boy and his mother.

Moments later, once reassured that the boy is conscious and in good hands, the crowd that has amassed at the intersection disperses and the cars stopped on either side also drive off. Peter and Hannah remain standing on the pavement with the boy and his mother.

—You talk to her, Hannah, Peter says. There's no way she'll understand my Arabic. Tell her he has to be taken to hospital.

—We'll have to take her, Peter. She won't be let in on her own.

Hannah turns to the boy's mother and explains the situation to her.

—No, the young woman exclaims, pointing to Peter. Let your husband treat him. We can't go to hospital.

—My husband can only do so much, Hannah says quietly. Your son needs to be properly checked.

The young woman reaches for her child; she picks him up and begins to walk away.

—She probably doesn't have any papers and is here illegally, Hannah says. She's afraid of getting into trouble if she goes for help. What should we do?

Peter frowns.

—I suppose we can take them over to our place for now, he tells Hannah. I can keep an eye on him there. It's better than letting them leave like this. Were there any other family members with them?

—There might have been but they ran away after the boy fell, says Hannah, shaking her head. I guess they were worried about getting into trouble if any policemen turned up.

She reaches for the woman's arm and explains that Peter wants to make sure the boy gets safely through the next couple of hours.

—You can come with us, Hannah says reassuringly. We won't go to the hospital. Don't be afraid. We only want to help.

Once at the apartment, Hannah and Peter lead the two into the living room and ask them to sit down but they remain standing in the doorway, looking hesitant.

Hannah squats down to speak to the boy.

—What's your name? she asks.

She is surprised at the intense blue of his eyes. His other features are difficult to make out since his face is covered with dirt. Hannah smiles encouragingly at him but he does not reply.

She stands up again and looks at the mother, who by now is trembling.

My God, Hannah thinks, she is a child herself. The

veil wrapped around her head is dark and frayed at the edges but her skin is clear and her features are delicate. Beneath the clear anxiety in her eyes, Hannah also sees diffidence, and thinks that perhaps the young mother is reluctant to give in too easily to her vulnerability.

—There's no need to be afraid, Hannah says. We only brought you here because my husband needs to observe your son for a few hours. It's important that he doesn't go to sleep. Do you understand?

The woman nods.

—We're not going to call the police, I promise. You don't even have to tell me your name. My name is Hannah.

—I'm Fatima, the young woman finally says.

—OK, Fatima. Just sit down and I'll get you something to eat.

—I'm going inside to change, Peter says. I'll be back in a bit to help you, sweetheart.

She makes sandwiches and brings them into the sitting room with a large bottle of water.

—Let me show you where the bathroom is. You can wash your hands there.

Fatima frowns.

—We haven't always been like this, you know, she suddenly blurts out. I kept a spotless house and my son was always clean.

—I'm sorry. Hannah feels instantly contrite.

—It's only since we had to leave home, Fatima continues, her voice rising and tears streaming down her face. We don't have a proper place to stay and things have been so difficult.

Hannah attempts to put an arm around Fatima and feels her flinch. The little boy begins to whimper too.

They all three stand still for a moment.

—The little one is probably hungry, Hannah finally says. Let's see if we can get him to eat something, shall we?

—I'll just take him in for a wash first, Fatima says coldly.

When Anas arrives a while later just as Peter is checking on the child again, Hannah tells him what has happened.

—Just tell the mother he's likely to have a bump on his head for a few days but he'll be fine, Peter says.

—We can't let them leave now, says Hannah. It's dark out and the child might get sick again. Surely we can ask her to stay here for the night?

—If you can persuade her to stay, it's fine by me.

Hannah turns to Anas with a look of despair and speaks to him in English.

—You talk to her, she says. She won't tell me much except that she's in Beirut with her son on her own and doesn't know where her parents are. I . . . . I think she's afraid we'll report her to the authorities and she'll be deported. Maybe she'd be more comfortable talking to you because you're from Syria too.

Anas introduces himself and at the sound of his voice, his familiar accent, Fatima is visibly relieved. She tells him that she arrived in Lebanon several months ago with members of her husband's family.

—What about your parents and siblings? Anas asks gently.

—They used to live on the outskirts of Damascus and escaped when their neighbourhood was taken over by rebels. I haven't heard from them since. I need to find them. Can you help me?

—We can try but you need to stay here tonight in case the little boy needs the doctor's help. Will you do that?

—Yes.

Once Fatima and her son are settled on a mattress on the living-room floor, Hannah and Peter talk in their room, as they prepare to sleep, of how they can help her further.

—The most important thing would be to get her back to her family, Peter says.

—They might be anywhere at this point. How are we going to find them?

—Maysoun might be able to help. But Fatima will have to be willing to provide her full name and identity card.

—Anas seems to have gained her trust. I'm sure he'll

be able to persuade her to do that. I'll talk to her again in the morning. She may be less resistant after a good night's sleep.

—I'll call Maysoun first thing then.

Peter smiles and smoothes back a lock of hair that has fallen over Hannah's eyes.

—So now we're looking for Fatima's family as well as Anas's?

—I suppose we are, he replies.

—I'm glad, Hannah says, leaning forward to kiss him.

She has sometimes wondered what it must be like for him, living here, in the midst of this turbulence, his past so remote and inaccessible. If he is here primarily because of her, then are there times when he might regret his decision to remain? From the start, she had told him she would not be willing to move to the United States, this despite the better prospects of work for him there, despite the obvious advantages of living in a country where he would enjoy full rights.

She had explained before they got married that in Lebanon women do not have the right to pass on citizenship to their spouses, and not being a citizen meant Peter could not practise medicine here. His solution to this problem had been to find a job as a consultant in an international organization that focused on matters of health. Although he has reassured her time and again that this is exactly the kind of work that gives him the most satisfaction, especially in view of the current situation, she worries now, after her recent conversation with Anas, that he may not have been completely honest with her about this.

And while she knows he has never been particularly close to his family, she suspects there must be a great deal that he misses about home: the relative ease and comfort of it; the room to breathe in relationships that do not so readily become demanding and perpetually binding. She knows also that there have been moments when he has been unsure of his place here, has seen in his eyes an expression of bewilderment at the circumstances that surround him, even a measure of impatience which scares her because it is unclear where it may lead. Once or twice in recent months, as the situation in the country has worsened, she has asked him if he ever has thoughts of leaving, and rather than completely deny it as he has done before, his reply was that he would never dream of leaving without her wanting to as well.

It occurs to her now that her position with Peter is not very different from that Anas faces with his wife, and while she cannot see him taking off and leaving her behind as Brigitte has done, she wonders if there will be a moment in the near future when their relationship too will be threatened by the events that surround them.

Yet she knows these troubling thoughts only come to her at night when she is a vague version of herself, the dark and silence scattering the bits of her that are strongest and most determined into the atmosphere like dust. This is how she waits impatiently for the day, for movement, for speech, for those, like herself, who wake up counting on something happening, one small thing that will reassure them once again that they are not alone.

—By the way, how was your trip to the encampments in the Bekaa? Peter asks. With everything going on I haven't asked about your work.

—It's going well, *habibi*. There is an overwhelming number of tragic stories to report on. It's heartbreaking. They're sending a photographer from England in a couple of weeks so I need to have everything sorted out by then.

—How many pieces do you have to write?

—At least two, I guess. The paper has commissioned articles about the camps in Jordan and Turkey as well.

—I would have thought with the number of refugees escaping to Europe now, there wouldn't be much interest in the West about what's going on in the Middle East.

—But that's exactly why they've asked for these articles. There hasn't been enough coverage of the millions of homeless Syrians in countries in the region.

Peter lies back on his pillow and looks at Hannah.

—I'm proud of you, sweetheart, he says as he closes his eyes. I just want you to know that.

She is suddenly aware of her heart beating and places a hand on her chest as if in an attempt to slow it down a little. She leans towards Peter and whispers in his ear.

—Thanks for your confidence in me, *habibi*.

But Peter is already fast asleep.

Chapter 9

Fatima sits on the floor in the living room with Wassim asleep in her lap. It is dark outside, Hannah and Peter have already gone to bed, and as she begins to recount her story Anas feels himself sink into a deep silence.

—The bombing was terrifying, she begins. They used all kinds of weapons on my husband's village, shot at us from aeroplanes, tanks and machine guns. We had no shelters to go to, nowhere to hide, and I knew if I didn't get out of there, we would be killed.

—I gathered a few of our things, picked Wassim up and left. There were lots of other people gathered in the streets and I joined my husband's family. We'd heard about villages elsewhere being bombed and held under siege, of people being starved inside their own homes or rounded up and slaughtered, and we knew we had to get away quickly.

She pauses and bends her head to look at her son.

—I lost my husband nearly four years ago, a few months after the war began. He was conscripted into the army and was killed very early on. I told myself at the time that I would not abandon our house, that I would hold on to it for Wassim no matter what, but that was not to be.

Fatima's narrative goes backwards and forwards in time and still Anas only listens.

—I never wanted to get married, she continues. I wanted to stay on at school but my father was adamant, said it was a good match and that he would be happy to get me off his hands. My husband was a good man and his family treated me well, but I was much happier when I was at home with my own family.

She looks into the distance and clears her throat.

—Anyway, we managed to get out of the village and made it across the border to the narrow strip of land between Syria and Lebanon. For a while, we stayed in a camp set up there by an aid agency but eventually moved on. My husband's uncle decided we should go south, to a village on the coast where he used to work for a wealthy Lebanese family that owns citrus groves. He said they might be able to help us, that the men would be able to get work and earn money to keep their families.

—At first I wanted to stay on at the camp on the border because I kept hoping that my parents would turn up and take me with them. When that didn't

happen I agreed to leave. What I didn't realize was
that we would be swapping one camp for another where
the conditions were just as bad.

Anas interrupts her at this point.

—So you don't know where your parents are?

She shakes her head.

—We weren't able to keep in touch because of the
fighting. I heard through someone at the border camp
that they had also left Syria but they have never been
in touch. I don't know how I ever thought they would
be able to find me.

Wassim stirs and she starts to rock him back and
forth in her arms.

—Do you have a wife? she suddenly asks Anas.

—Yes, I do, he replies. I have a son too, and a
daughter.

—Why aren't they here with you?

—I'm only here for a short while, for work. We
live in Damascus.

—You left them there?

—That's where our home is, he says, the irritation
he is suddenly feeling in his voice.

She looks at him and says nothing.

—Anyway, he continues, they've left now.

—Where to?

He decides to redirect the conversation to her account.

—What brought you to Beirut?

She blinks and avoids looking directly at him.

—I thought you said you went down south with your husband's people, Fatima?

She leans over and hands him the little boy, then gets up and walks to the other side of the living room where Hannah put down a mattress and some pillows and blankets earlier. Anas carries Wassim over to the mattress and puts him down, pulling the covers up over him _ and gently caressing the top of his head. For a moment, he is reminded of his own children and feels a sudden sharp pain in his chest at the thought.

—You're missing your own son, aren't you? she asks once Anas stands up again. You don't know where your family is either.

They are standing very close to each other now, her voice low though not menacing. She puts a hand on his arm and leans into him so that he has to shift on his legs to steady himself.

—I could tell you would understand, she says with urgency. The moment you came in this evening, I knew I could trust you. The others are kind but they don't know what it's like for us.

Her face is very close to his and he feels a strong desire to step away but does not for fear of offending her.

—You're mistaken, he says. My wife and children have just gone away for a short while, to her family in Europe.

—They're safe then?

75

He nods.

—But you're upset that they left, aren't you?

He purses his lips and does not reply.

—They're better off wherever they are, believe me, she says. Anyone who has a chance to leave Syria and doesn't is a fool. Will you see them again soon?

—I hope so, Anas replies.

Her eyes flicker, as if something has just occurred to her.

—Then you have to help me, please, she says, still leaning against him.

—What is it?

—There's another child. I . . . I came to Beirut to have her so that the family wouldn't find out. I can't possibly keep her. Please, you have to take her. You and your wife can take care of her.

He shakes her hand off his arm, alarmed at what she has told him.

—You've just had a baby? I thought you said your husband was dead.

He is unmoved when she begins to cry.

—Where is this baby? What have you done with her?

He moves away to sit down, wondering if he has still to hear the worst of it.

—Please. She is pleading with him now. Please listen to what I have to say before you make up your mind.

She looks so miserable that he feels suddenly ashamed

of himself for reacting so violently and motions for her to join him on the living-room sofa.

—Tell me, he says quietly, his heart beating less urgently now, his mind clearing.

*

Later, lying on the bed in the spare room, he reminds himself that Fatima's is hardly an unusual story. As the war in Syria goes into its fifth year, over four million people have already fled into neighbouring countries – Lebanon, Turkey, Iraq and Jordan – or made the long and perilous journey further on to Europe. Many of them, he knows, have faced still greater hardship than this young woman, but he is nonetheless moved by her plight, wishes somehow to honour her truthfulness with his own, wonders how his own circumstances coincide with hers.

There are different ways of being a refugee, different expressions of displacement and dissonance, depending on the point at which we begin our experience of dislocation, the point at which our lives are first disrupted by the violence imposed on us by events that seem outside our control.

Perhaps for Fatima, the experience has been something like stepping out of one black hole and falling straight into another that is deeper and darker because it is unknowable, something like losing your past and not having a vision of the future to sustain you through the present.

When he married Brigitte, Anas had not reckoned on the dilemma that he would eventually face as a result. He sees now that in refusing her plea that they go into voluntary exile, he has inadvertently made refugees of himself and of his family, though ones obviously in a position of privilege.

Like Fatima and millions of others, he has already lost the certainty of home, of belonging, and, in seeking refuge elsewhere, is imposing on the entitlement of others. He feels suddenly and intensely the oppression of his predicament, the want in it of dignity and expectation.

Chapter 10

The south of Lebanon is resplendent with flowers in spring: white and yellow daisies, crocuses, poppies and baby's breath on green hills that dip towards the pungent sea, with, on the way, orchards of lemons and oranges and fields of banana trees nearly meeting the water. But although it is comforting, Hannah thinks, to know that the seasons and their fruits continue as before, it is not a perfect vista.

The highway on either side is littered with rubbish – empty soft drink cans, plastic bags and tissue paper – while in some places small mounds of it lie smouldering in the sun. She sees a man with two large hessian bags slung over his shoulders picking up whatever is recyclable, his clothes and load covered with dust, his head bent to the task as cars whizz past dangerously close. To the left, where once there were terraces of trees and bush, are rows of low-rise buildings, many grey and unfinished, shoddy constructions that house some of the tens of thousands displaced by Israel's twenty-year occupation of vast areas of the south, and who have, since the liberation in 2000, nonetheless remained.

As each conflict has developed and eventually made way for the next, waves of migrants have followed in its wake; the human make-up of this country, this region, is constantly changing, loyalties forever unfixed, and those left behind, whether Lebanese or Palestinian, whether from Syria, Iraq, Libya or Yemen, find themselves disconnected and dependent on whatever and whomever provides reprieve from this state of drifting. Is dispossession exclusive to the poor and destitute or are we all in the same situation now?

The Lebanon into which our ancestors were born was part of an Ottoman Empire that did not recognize it as an independent nation. After the end of the First World War and the defeat of the Turks, European leaders divided up the region into mandates which they ruled and used to expand their spheres of influence, and the Lebanon that eventually came into being included numerous religious communities in different parts of the country for whom the idea of unity meant little.

Ours has always been a region of shifting identities, so what exactly does it mean to be Lebanese? This horrific war and its repercussions on Lebanon are putting our existence as a viable nation into question.

Hannah sighs and glances at Fatima and her young son asleep on the back seat beside her. It had not been easy at first to persuade her to tell them where she and Wassim had been living. When Hannah began to suspect that Fatima had no intention of leaving the apartment, the young woman had finally relented and told them what they wanted to know.

—We've been staying in an encampment with my husband's family in the south, in a village not far from Tyre.

—But what are you doing here in Beirut? Hannah asked.

Fatima's expression was sullen.

—I have a place to stay at the Bourj al-Barajneh Palestinian camp. I have relatives there. I'll go back as soon as Wassim starts to feel better. You don't have to worry about me.

Hannah was at a loss how to make the younger woman understand that she was only trying to help.

—Wassim is already better, Fatima, she said gently. I just want to make sure you get back safely to your family. Is that where your husband's relatives are, in the south?

Fatima nodded.

—Then we'll take you there as soon as possible. You shouldn't have to make the journey on your own.

Now, after making sure Wassim still has his seatbelt on despite his reclining position, Hannah leans forward towards the front seat where Anas is sitting by the taxi driver. She taps him on the shoulder.

—I'll wake her up when we get closer to our destination, she says quietly. She'll have to show us the way.

Anas smiles and nods his assent.

—Not far now, I think, he tells her. We're already
on the outskirts of Sidon. It'll take us another twenty
minutes or so to get to Tyre.

Hannah leans back in her seat and looks out of the
window again. She is aware of a feeling of discomfort
growing inside her but cannot quite place it. This not
knowing, this uncertainty will only lead to further
anxiety, she knows. She takes a deep breath, closes her
eyes and tries to focus only on her breathing, tries to
push the fear away.

*

In Tyre, Fatima directs them to a small field on the
outside of a village, a couple of kilometres from the
sea. They take a right turn on to a dirt road, come to
a stop at the end of it and get out of the car. Ahead
of them are a dozen or so canvas tents on either side
of a narrow concrete pathway. On one side of each of
the tents is a large, plastic barrel that Hannah assumes
contains water and further along, grouped together in
a corner of the field, are a number of small, portable
cabins. Hannah sighs with relief: at least they have some
degree of sanitation.

She watches as Wassim runs ahead of them and

disappears into one of the tents. Presently, a man dressed in a dark grey *gallabiyyah* that falls down to his ankles emerges from the tent and begins to walk towards them. As he gets closer, Hannah notes his skin is weathered by the sun and his moustache is peppered with grey. Wrapped around his head is the traditional black and white headscarf worn by the inhabitants of rural regions of Syria and Palestine.

Fatima rushes towards him and takes his hand.

—*Ammi*, she greets him respectfully.

He gives her a brief hug.

—Where have you been, *ya binti*, he says pulling away again to look at her. Your cousin at the Bourj al-Barajneh camp sent a message asking about you and we've been very worried.

—It's Wassim, she replies, her voice trembling a little. He had an accident and these people took care of us.

—An accident? What happened?

—He's fine now, *Ammou*. Please don't worry.

As if to prove her point, Wassim runs out of the tent followed by a motley group of barefoot children who gather around to stare at Anas and Hannah.

Anas reaches out to shake the man's hand and introduces himself. Hannah follows suit.

—*Ahlan*, Fatima's uncle says. Welcome to you both.

Hannah feels a hand grab hers and looks down into the face of a little girl of about six, her hair pulled back in a pony tail, her eyes dark and tender.

She smiles and reaches out to pat the child on the head.

—Hello, Hannah says and the little girl squeezes her hand a little harder.

Fatima's uncle leads them towards the entrance of the tent he came out of earlier but Hannah's companion tries to pull her past it.

Hannah signals to Anas, tells him she'll join him in a minute and follows the little girl to another tent further down the path. She bends down to get inside and hesitates for a moment until her eyes adjust to the darkness. The little girl points to Hannah's shoes.

—Take them off, she says.

Hannah slips off her shoes and feels the smooth surface of the thin, straw carpet beneath her feet. In one corner of the tent, the concrete floor is bare and a young woman squats next to a little boy, rubbing vigorously at his head with a towel. Beside them is a circular tin tub filled with soapy water.

The young woman looks up, notices Hannah's presence and her hands go up to her uncovered head.

—Oh!

The little boy slips away from his mother.

—Bassem, come back here, the woman shouts at him. I still have to comb your hair.

—I'm sorry, Hannah blurts out. I shouldn't have come in without calling out first.

The woman smiles and reaches for a scarf which she wraps around her head.

—That's all right, she says. I can see Leila brought you with her. She loves to bring visitors.

Hannah laughs.

—Yes, but not in the middle of bathtime!

—Leila, bring your brother back here and comb his hair before he gets it dirty again, the mother calls to the little girl.

She motions for Hannah to sit down beside her on a long cushion on the floor.

The inside of the tent is small but neat and Hannah is also impressed by its cleanliness. There are thin cushions for seats lined against one wall of what must be the living room and a single gas burner placed on a slab of wood not far from the area the little boy had bathed in with plates and cups stacked next to it. The kitchen, she supposes.

Leila comes back in with her brother in tow and carrying a pink backpack that she hands to Hannah.

—She wants to show you her schoolwork, the mother says.

Hannah unzips the bag and takes out a worn notebook which Leila asks her to open. Inside is the unmistakable, unsteady writing of a child, the letters of the alphabet, in English and in Arabic, looking like drawings rather than mere symbols of sounds. She imagines Leila's small head bent in an arc towards the page, a pencil in her hand, her mouth perhaps twitching a little as she attempts to reproduce an approximation of the letter. Though she knows the little girl is waiting for her reaction, Hannah is too moved to speak at first.

—This is wonderful, she says finally, reaching out to cup Leila's face with her hand. You are a very clever little girl, aren't you?

She turns to the mother.

—I'm glad to see she's going to school.

—Well, she did the first few months we were here. She studied at a public school in a nearby village but she's since had to stop.

—But why? Hannah asks. Public schools are free here. I know they've been trying hard to accommodate children from Syria.

The young woman looks at her for a moment and then smiles. Hannah notes compassion in her eyes and is surprised by that.

—We could no longer afford to pay for the bus that takes her to and from school, the woman says gently. I'm trying to teach her here at home, though. She loves to learn. She points to a low wall of loose bricks piled on top of one another where Hannah can make out letters scratched on to the stone.

—Your husband isn't able to find work?

—He's working in an orchard not far from here at the moment. It's picking season for oranges and lemons. Once that ends, we're not sure what he'll be able to do.

Hannah wants to tell her that Syria has provided cheap labour for the construction industry in Lebanon for years.

—Surely there's plenty of manual work out there for him, she says instead, realizing that she might be coming across as patronizing.

The woman continues to smile at her.

—He needs a residence visa now and we don't have the money to pay for it. There are new regulations for Syrian refugees living here.

—I don't understand. I didn't know any laws had been introduced. I thought the borders were open and people could come and go as they pleased.

—Why would you know? the woman says kindly. They don't apply to you. The regulations require that we pay for a residence visa and also that we won't try to work here. Very few people are able to comply with the law and without valid papers the authorities have the right to send us back to Syria. It's happened to several families already.

There is no sarcasm in her voice, though Hannah cannot tell if what she can sense in it is acceptance or resignation. Once again, she feels a burrowing sadness within, finds herself suffering the same discomfort in her chest she had felt earlier, her heart beating faster and faster until she thinks it might burst.

After a moment, she reaches for her handbag and takes out her purse.

—I'd like to help, she says. Please let me do that. It's the least I can do.

—Yes, replies the young woman matter-of-factly, her expression open and unashamed.

*

When, a little later, she joins Anas in the tent with Fatima and her family, Hannah finds them sitting on the floor drinking coffee. A woman pours out a cup and hands it to her.

Anas turns to Hannah and smiles.

—Abou Ahmad and Oum Ahmad insisted on extending their hospitality to us. This is Hannah, he continues. She's the wife of the doctor who looked after Wassim.

—May Allah keep you and your family safe. Oum Ahmad smiles at Hannah.

—I'm just glad we were there at the time, Hannah replies. Those intersections are very dangerous, especially at night.

Abou Ahmad clears his throat and looks directly at Anas.

—You're a fellow Syrian and I can be open with you. I'm not proud that I have to send the women and children out asking for money from strangers on the streets but what choice do we have? I get manual work occasionally but it's not enough to keep us going. Our position here has become very precarious.

—Have you registered with the UN agency for refugees? Hannah asks. Surely, they can help you.

—We did that as soon as we arrived, but aid from the agency has been cut drastically and we get very little help now.

His wife interrupts him.

—Last time he went out looking for work, he was stopped by the authorities and taken to jail because his papers weren't in order, she says. They beat him and kept him there for two days. I thought they'd sent him back to Syria.

Abou Ahmad looks embarrassed.

—That's enough, he tells her. Then, turning to Anas once again, he continues: I just don't have the money for our visas. We already pay the landowner here rent. He shakes his head.

—We understand, Anas says quietly.

—It's impossible here, Oum Ahmad says. We'd be better off taking our lives into our own hands and running away to Germany like others have done.

—It's a dangerous trip, Hannah says. Many have died on the way.

—What do we have to lose? the woman asks. Look at the way we're living now. We had homes and property once. We weren't rich but we managed, our men worked and our children went to school.

When they get up to leave, Hannah watches Anas take Abou Ahmad aside and hand the older man some money. She turns away so as not to embarrass him further and calls to Fatima.

—We have to go now, Fatima, Hannah says quietly.

The young woman pulls at Hannah's arm until they're outside the tent. She hands Hannah a piece of paper.

—This is a copy of my identity card, she says. The artist said you would need it to find my family.

—I hope we can. We're definitely going to try.

Fatima looks behind her towards the tent and moves closer to Hannah.

—I don't want my uncle to know about this, she says in a low voice.

—I understand. I'll let you know as soon as we've heard anything.

On the way home, the look on Fatima's face as she bade her goodbye returns to her. There was too much hope in it, Hannah thinks, closing her eyes.

Chapter 11

In leaving Iraq, Maysoun knows she also left behind the most vital period in her life when the dual struggles for love and for survival had dominated her every thought.

During the bombing of Baghdad in 1991, which lasted for forty consecutive days, Maysoun and her mother had endured forty sleepless nights side by side in the bed in which her father had taken his last breath, their hands lightly touching as if to confirm their togetherness, their breathing strangely quiet for fear the mere sense of it would lead the carnage to them. Then, getting up to daylight, dazed from lack of sleep or from awe at still being alive, they would go out into the heavy air, into the black soot rained down on them by the Western allies that covered the streets and houses with its greyness, and laid waste to the living, to trees that would never bear fruit again, to people whose health would not recover, to a country capitulated.

Once the bombing stopped, what followed, Maysoun discovered, was to be even more difficult to endure. The sanctions that were meant to weaken the regime impoverished the Iraqi people even further while at the same time served to fill the pockets of the dictator and his cronies.

Maysoun's mother held down a menial job just to make ends meet while Maysoun herself searched for work in vain; there was no place in the new order for the educated youth. Bit by bit, and like so many others, the two women began to sell off their jewellery, those pieces that had made up her mother's dowry as well as the beautiful gold bangles that Maysoun's grandmother had given her for her coming of age. Walking through the old souks looking for buyers, Maysoun's eyes would fill with tears at the sight of people peddling their precious belongings: rare books and antique furniture, family heirlooms, pots and pans, clothing and household goods, anything that could hold destitution at bay even briefly.

Then in the midst of an unprecedented crime wave brought on by the collapse of civil society and its institutions, as the residents of one of ancient Mesopotamia's most revered cities reeled at the sudden viciousness of some of its residents, Maysoun found love at a small get-together organized by one of her friends.

Kamel had just completed his studies in medicine and had decided, he told her, not to practise in protest at a presidential decree that doctors, engineers and other professionals be forbidden from leaving the country.

—Would you believe me if I told you I have an American passport? he began in a seductive voice, made tipsy by drinking. My parents, after emigrating to the United States when my siblings and I were very young, decided, in their wisdom, to return. I was thirteen at the time and had begun to think of American suburbia as home.

She felt restrained energy in him, warmth radiating from his dark skin that made her want to get closer, that drew her in.

—But why would your parents come back here when everyone is trying to run away? she asked, astonished.

He put his head back and laughed out loud.

—They did not want us to grow up knowing nothing about our background, our home country.

She smelled the alcohol in his breath, the rich scent of aniseed and spirits.

—Then the situation here turned bad, of course, he continued, and my father decided to move to Libya where he had found a job. By then, I was halfway through medical school and had no choice but to stay on here and finish.

93

For a moment, she felt as though they were alone
in the room.

—And now the authorities won't allow you to leave,
she said quietly. You're trapped just like the rest of us,
despite your foreign passport.

They stood very close together and, because he was
only a little taller than she was, Maysoun looked directly
into his eyes, saw in them, alongside the haziness
brought on by drink, unmistakable anguish, and felt
suddenly embarrassed at her longing to embrace a man
who until a few moments before had been a complete
stranger.

—You're blushing, he said softly. It's sweet.

—I . . . I'm sorry.

He smiled and leaned in to whisper in her ear.

—I feel the connection too, Maysoun.

When it was time for her to leave, Kamel took her
hand, called to a couple of his friends to join him, and
drove her home.

—I'll pick you up tomorrow, early evening, he told
her as she prepared to get out of the car. You go on
now. We'll just hang on here until you get safely inside.

How is she to describe what followed? Though she
knows well the story's end, where would the telling
have to begin to reveal its true meaning?

He had been her refuge, her light and darkness, a
source of unending love and a possessor of innate
wisdom unexpected in one so young. He was friend

and brother, as tender in his lovemaking as he was in the humdrum interactions of everyday life, so expansive of heart that with him she had felt her horizons open up to a world unlike anything she could have imagined, where there was the possibility of being at the centre of all that is good and complete and still survive in the midst of disorder and decay, of having the choice to live magnificently.

It seemed to her sometimes that they spent more time talking than anything else, alone together in his house, walking down the street, with friends and at every opportunity, conversations that not only rejuvenated her but served also to reconfigure her notion of self, as though these words exchanged contained within them a cure for low self-worth, helped make cohesive in her what had once been untold.

Yet, throughout the relationship, she had also been aware of her own role as observer of Kamel's increasing despair, a tilting of his equilibrium that was fuelled by heartbreak over the situation as well as a growing dependence on alcohol. When demonstrations by young men who believed in the promises of support for insurgence made to them by Western politicians began to take place around the country, their bravery was met with brutal repression within and complete silence without. Hearing of the disappearance of two of his cousins, Kamel felt greater anguish and told Maysoun he would have to find a way to escape Iraq before things got worse still. He said he could not bear this state of affairs any longer.

—You will come with me, my darling, he said. I'll take you to America with me and we'll be together always.

A year or so later, Kamel was shot and killed for the few dollars he kept in his bedside drawer, the murderer one of the friends he had introduced her to the night he and Maysoun had met.

Going on had seemed impossible at first but the worsening situation and concern for her mother's welfare prevented Maysoun from breaking down. She began to investigate how they might leave the country, perhaps crossing the border to Syria and then seeking refuge somewhere in Europe or even as far away as America or New Zealand where many fellow Iraqis had settled after the war. But a presidential decision forbidding women from travelling unless accompanied by a male guardian made escape impossible, since Maysoun had neither the connections nor the money to bribe her away across the border in defiance of the new law.

If she had thought Kamel's dying would be the end of her, then she could not have anticipated the humiliations and horrors that followed, could not have seen herself endure a week's incarceration by the police during their investigation of his murder, would not have felt herself die and come back to life again on her release. In moments of emotional lucidity, she admits that Kamel's anguish and alcoholism might eventually have destroyed her too had he remained alive, but even that thought does not help assuage a grief that, years later, continues to burn inside her.

As it was, soon after Kamel's killer was put on trial and convicted, Maysoun was offered a job with the International Red Cross, one of several relief organizations entrusted with the implementation of the Oil-for-Food Programme introduced by the United Nations to relieve the plight of the Iraqi population. It seemed to her then that what life had taken away from her with one hand, it was giving back with the other, uneven though the equation was. When she was given the opportunity to transfer to the office in Beirut, she thought she would have to turn it down at first because her mother refused to leave with her.

—You need to go, her mother said, and make a proper life for yourself elsewhere, Maysoun. Go live your life and leave me here. This is where I will always belong.

Since then, Maysoun regularly sends money to her mother, telephones her on a weekly basis and has been back to see her twice since her departure.

Perhaps, Maysoun tells herself, it is not injustice we continue to suffer but the ambiguity that lies beyond it, the interval between insurmountable distress and that moment which falls short of finding inner peace.

*

Looking at her computer screen, Maysoun glimpses New Zealand from the terrace of Jalal's home, an expanse of deep and differing shades of green that she has never seen elsewhere, damp air visible as light fog, faint outlines of a city in the distance and what seems like infinite room to breathe.

—Can you see the view? he asks. Are you there, Maysoun?

—Yes, yes, I'm still here. It's beautiful, just as you described it.

Jalal's face appears on the computer screen again.

—It's been raining today, that's why the view isn't too clear, he says, smiling. Usually, when the weather's good, we can see all the way to the ocean.

—It looks so clean. I can almost smell the freshness in the air.

—Makes a change from the diesel fumes of Beirut, doesn't it?

Maysoun laughs.

—Yes, it does, she says.

It gives her pleasure to look at him, the warmth in his eyes, his face so familiar that she can make out the changing years in it, the boisterous, outgoing boy she had known as a child not far beneath the kind man with greying temples that he has become.

A relative on her father's side of the family, Jalal had lived only a few streets away in Baghdad, and had been, along with his two younger sisters, a frequent visitor to the house as a child; he came to play along-side Maysoun in her beloved garden and, like her, sought shade beneath the floating fragrance of the *naranj* trees.

He had left Baghdad to study abroad and when he returned, married and had two children. Maysoun kept in touch with Jalal and his family throughout this period, during the First Gulf War and then his young wife's illness with cancer and her untimely death. But when the prospect of another American attack on Iraq became real in 2003, he decided to leave, taking his children and sisters with him. She did not hear from him for several years but in recent months, they have recon-nected through video calls and they have been speaking regularly.

—How are things in Beirut? he asks her. It must be getting more and more difficult for you there, having to cope on your own.

—I'm doing good work here, Jalal. As you know, we're dealing with a terrible refugee crisis now.

—Yes, of course. I know you are. I'm just concerned about you. After all that's happened in your life, maybe it's time you took it easy and started taking better care of yourself.

—Jalal, even speaking in Arabic, you're sounding like a Westerner now. How can I take it easy when things are so bad here and need our attention?

He shakes his head.

—Why do you always feel you should suffer along with others, Maysoun?

—That's not what I meant.

—Perhaps it isn't, he says after a pause. I was actually going to ask you to think about coming out here for a while, to see how you like it. There's a small but very active Iraqi community in Auckland and I think you would fit in well.

—Fit in? What do you mean?

—Just that you might want to stay on, that's all. Finally get away from that troubled part of the world and discover how different life can be.

She tries to imagine what life abroad would be like, imagines the certainty in it and, during moments of aloneness, a yearning for connection. It is inconceivable to her, the idea of being so far away, though she is not sure quite what this might mean since she is no longer home. She admits that even if she were to return to Iraq, it would never again be the country that had once granted her fortitude and purpose.

She remembers walking to school earlier than usual one morning – she would have been no more than eight or nine at the time — when the leather satchel that she carried on her back suddenly came open and all the books, notebooks and pencils in it fell to the ground. The street was empty, the children she usually encountered on her way not there at that hour, and, bending down to retrieve her things, Maysoun had felt, perhaps for the first time, the sensation of being entirely alone.

For a moment, she thought she heard the trees murmur her name and felt the wind nudging at her, its touch on the small of her back gentle but insistent. Maysoun, Maysoun, the trees called as her body suddenly lifted itself off the ground and hovered there, her breath expanding to take in the street and all the houses in it, embracing the trees and the surrounding air, containing in it all that she knew, her life so far and what was to come, the love she would encounter, and, further in the distance, fears that would not prove fearful, solitude without loneliness, communion with the spirit, a final acceptance and a willingness to keep.

—Maysoun? Can you hear me?

Jalal's voice wakes her from her reverie.

—Yes, yes. I'm here. She smiles to reassure him.

—Will you at least consider paying us a visit here sometime soon?

It is entirely possible, thinks Maysoun, that we only happen upon home once in this lifetime and that my chance has already come and gone. What then would I have to lose in leaving again?

—Of course I will, she tells Jalal. I'll definitely think about it.

Chapter 12

Anas ponders, as they sit waiting in the restaurant, how he might best depict the steel-grey colour the man had worn, the suggestion of a taut body underneath, the scarf coiled on top of his head, the way his eyes moved restlessly as he spoke, and the mixture of dignity and defencelessness in his manner. Anas moves the empty plate in front of him to another corner of the table and begins to draw imaginary lines with his fingers on to the white tablecloth, shapes that mimic the waves of emotion inside him, the ups and downs of his sadness and perhaps something of God's grace looking on.

From the corner of one eye, he notes that Hannah and Maysoun are watching him carefully but it is easy enough for him to ignore their attention. Once the idea for a piece takes shape in his head, there is no letting go of it, no distraction that can interrupt the flow. He pinches the tablecloth here and there to create peaks on its surface, the neatly ironed cotton stiff to the touch at first but eventually pliable. It reminds him of clay in some ways, its initial resistance and then the satisfaction of feeling it bend to his will.

Painting or sculpture, he is not certain yet which this will be, but he can feel something forming already, something that will live inside him for some time before it can come into physical being.

—Anas.

He feels a hand on his shoulder and looks up to see Peter smiling down at him. He moves further along the table to make room for his friend.

—Sit down, *habibi*. We've been waiting for you.

—Where are the ladies? Peter asks.

Anas looks around in surprise. The two chairs where the women were sitting earlier are empty.

—I didn't see them leave.

Peter chuckles and points to the bar where Hannah and Maysoun are ordering drinks.

—You were too involved with the creative process to notice what was going on around you, weren't you?

Anas smiles sheepishly.

—You know me well, he says.

—So what are you conjuring up this time, my friend?

—It's this man we met, Fatima's uncle. There's something about him.

—What exactly?

—I'm not sure. He seemed to be the nominal head

of the encampment, a group of about fifteen or so families – dozens of children running around in bare feet, the women too, not too shy about letting themselves be seen, and young men hanging around looking listless.

—The leader by virtue of his age, you mean?

Anas shakes his head.

—I mean they all stood around waiting for him to speak and really listened when he did, making the occasional comment but not interrupting his flow for more than a moment. He had an air of refinement about him that stuck out in that environment, you know? If I really wanted to pinpoint what it was that captured my attention I'd need to go back to see him . . .

He hesitates.

—I'm in two minds about that, though. What if my original impression is tarnished by a second visit?

—But I thought you had to study your subjects very closely before painting or sculpting them, Peter says. Surely it's a process.

—That's just it, you see, Anas replies. Sometimes it takes only a moment or two for a person or a situation to have that kind of impact, to stir my interest and demand that I do something about it. The rest, the time it takes to actually make something of it, represents only my interaction with it, my perception of what I saw and felt.

—Hello, there.

Maysoun and Hannah return to the table carrying four bottles of chilled beer between them.

—Excellent, Peter exclaims. Exactly what I need after a hard day at work.

Hannah hands him a beer and reaches out to touch his hand.

—Is Anas talking about that man again?

Peter nods.

—He's besotted with him, it seems.

Maysoun joins in.

—From what I've heard so far, he must be really something, she says. To be Anas's latest muse, I mean.

Anas looks at their faces, sees the entirety of them but also, with his artist's eye, notes individual features, the different shades of dejection and its opposite hopefulness, and though he tries hard to discern behind their expressions a common bond, he sees only himself.

Hannah interrupts his thoughts.

—It's what he told us about their situation that was so upsetting. This law the government recently introduced is making life really difficult for the refugees.

—Yes, I know, Maysoun replies. It demands a list of requirements for residence here that are virtually impossible for them to fulfil, including proof of accommodation and a Lebanese sponsor, as well as sworn affidavits that they will not seek employment. It's a poorly orchestrated strategy to try to stem the tide of refugees.

—But when they're officially registered with the United Nations, doesn't that mean they're here legally? And don't they get some kind of financial help?

—They did get plenty of help in the beginning, both financial and otherwise, explains Maysoun. The UN commission on refugees played a part, and so did local communities and non-profits. But funds have been severely depleted, and the truth is that the longer the conflict continues, the worse the situation will become for them.

—It's heartbreaking.

—Yes, it is, agrees Maysoun, but it's also true that this country is simply too small and too unstable to continue to provide safe harbour for nearly two million refugees.

—But other countries in the region are taking them.

—Turkey and Jordan have taken in hundreds of thousands but they've closed their doors to them now. The truth is nobody wants them, especially not with the rise of the Islamic State.

—And now the exodus towards Europe . . .

There is a pause in the conversation, their heads filled with images they have seen in the news of refugees risking their lives in lifeboats on the Mediterranean, the long journey towards central Europe, often on foot and across hostile borders, to a future unknown but still better than that which they had left behind.

Maysoun shrugs.

—Governments and people in the West are not exactly enamoured with Muslims at the moment. Germany is the only country that has admitted to a responsibility for them.

Hannah frowns.

—The real truth is that had these refugees been white and Christian, European countries would have welcomed them with open arms, she says. This is as much about racism as it is about war and the inevitable movement of people away from it.

—Has anyone heard about the group that's planning a vigil in Washington? Peter asks. They're going to stand in front of the White House and take turns reciting the names of all those killed in the war in Syria. I wonder how long it'll take them to read out over a quarter of a million names.

He pauses.

—It's not as if the act will bring anyone back to life, but there's something in it, don't you think?

An image comes to Anas of a scroll unfolding on which words, in the loops, arcs and elegant contours of the Arabic script he loves, appear, and then suddenly extricate themselves and escape towards open skies, shadows released, a history of words and a confident belief in their power to change what is intolerable.

—It may be true that no one wants the refugees – Hannah returns to the original discussion – but they're happy to see the conflict in Syria continue. It's a convenient place for them to fight their little wars.

—Please, Hannah, Peter says. Let's not start this whole conspiracy theory against Arabs thing again.

—That's not what I'm saying at all, she protests. There's no denying that this war is accommodating internal as well as regional and international conflicts. Someone is training Islamic State fighters and providing them with weapons. As for the Syrian government, it's very clear who its supporters are. There are lots of interests at stake here, including those of Israel and its allies in the West.

—You're right, Hannah, Peter interrupts her. We all know this isn't merely about Syrians fighting among themselves, or even about a sectarian conflict between Sunni Islam and Shia Islam. I just think it's time the Arab world took some responsibility for the mess it finds itself in.

He shakes his head before continuing.

—It's just so frustrating. Look at what's going on around you, for heaven's sake. It's forty years since Lebanon's civil war began, over twenty since it ended, and this country is worse off now than it ever was. And after all the protests, the deaths that occurred in Egypt, the promises made, another dictator is in power there today. Not to mention the war in Yemen, the fighting in Libya, and the mayhem, oppression and displacement everywhere else. As for the Palestinians, how far have they got in their struggle to regain their homeland and who among their Arab brothers is willing to help them? It's an unholy mess, I'm telling you, and sometimes I wish I were much further away from it.

Hannah looks at him, her mouth open.

—Is that really how you feel? she asks.

The others remain silent, waiting for Peter's reply.

—You're surprised that I want to get away from all this madness, that I feel so frustrated at what's going on? Peter continues, his face turning red.

—What shocks me is that you now seem to be on the outside looking in, she says, looking pained. I always thought you considered yourself one of us.

—That's what you understood from what I just said, that I'm betraying you and this country in some way? His voice is harsh and uncompromising. Why can't I talk frankly about what I see happening around me? he continues. Does being an American mean I have to keep quiet or that I won't be accepted into this society any more?

—No, of course that's not it.

—Then what do you mean, Hannah? he asks quietly now. You don't think I belong here any more?

—Surely that's not what you're trying to say, Hannah? Maysoun intervenes.

But Hannah does not reply to the question.

—*Habibi*, Anas says after a long pause. I don't think

I've ever seen you so worked up before. Yours is usually the voice of reason amongst us hotheaded Arabs.

This makes Peter smile and the tension in the air dissipates somewhat.

—Let's order and eat, says Maysoun.

Peter turns to Hannah.

—I'm sorry. I didn't mean to shout.

—I know you didn't, she says, reaching out to touch his arm.

—If you ask me, Anas says, laughing, this kind of outburst must mean you're turning into one of us. God help you!

Chapter 13

In her parents' home, Brigitte is temporarily cocooned. There is love here but it is a quiet, contained sort of love, deep yet without the appendages of passion and guilt. She recalls this gentle detachment as the principal setting of a childhood that was not without its pain but which was nonetheless largely peaceful. Growing up in a country that would undergo profound change and prove up to that challenge, she sees now that she had been given enough freedom to discover the hidden rewards of solitude, to liken separateness to affection. And if her subsequent experiences proved to be the exact opposite, if the persistent intensity of her Damascus existence, the example of loving she met with there, contrasted wholly with that of home, she wills herself now into a more neutral state of being, feels herself suspended in time, finally finding release.

But there are moments when she cannot stop thinking

about Anas, when his face, pale and drawn, follows her wherever she goes, and she finds herself wondering whether in disappearing like this she may have irreparably broken his trust. At other times, she sees clearly the ways in which their confidence in each other had been shaken long before, so that when she is being honest with herself, she must also acknowledge that had war not broken out she would, with time, have found a thousand other reasons to leave the place that seemed reluctant to accept her as she was.

The prospect of settling in Damascus after they married had seemed exciting: for Anas because that was where his family lived and also since the city was a major source of inspiration for his work; and for Brigitte, at twenty-three, because she felt ready to venture further, to discover a part of the world that had always seemed not only mysterious but also slightly forbidding to her. Yet, young and passionately in love as she was, she had also been astute enough to understand that although her new husband was a member of an established, middle-class Christian community in Syria, he was nonetheless the product of a culture that was vastly different from her own.

The experience had been exactly as she had expected it to be in the first few years of her marriage: interesting and providing so much to discover, challenging, beautiful, and moving too at times; an environment not easy to blend into, in part because of her physical appearance, but one that was largely accepting, bemused by rather than rejecting of her. And if her in-laws proved to be more interfering than she would have liked, if what she perceived as her personal affairs were construed as concerns for the whole family to ponder and deal with, this was not the real reason behind her estrangement from her husband.

How to articulate it? she now thinks. If someone were to ask her what had happened between them, how would she explain what had started as a mere inkling, a seemingly inconsequential perception of distance that kept repeating itself until days would be wholly consumed by it, and nights too? When lying in bed together, the vacant hush of sleep made their separateness seem more marked, their loneliness heavier.

Resolving to talk to Anas about these misgivings she had made an unexpected visit to his studio one morning, climbing slowly up the stairs to the scent of jasmine and the sound of tree leaves rustling. Then, quietly pushing the big, wooden door open, she stepped inside. Stillness pervaded the entrance hall where Anas's jacket hung on a hook by the door, the kitchen with its uneven floor tiles, the sink and its old-fashioned iron tap just visible from where she stood, and, as she turned right to stand in the doorway of the studio proper, she had a perception of complete silence. A ray of light briefly blinded her. Blinking, she caught clear sight of him bent over a piece of sculpture on the table before him, his beautiful hands immersed in it, an outline of light and colour surrounding this shape that she knew was Anas but which now felt unfamiliar and otherworldly; in that moment before he looked up and became aware of her presence, she experienced a sense of disconnection so strong that she had had to grab on to the door frame to keep from falling, until recognition returned and it was her beloved husband who reached out to steady her, who took her in his arms.

But she does not want now to think too long on the past, does not want to doubt her actions, is anxious to focus on the task at hand, on finding out what the options open to her may be.

They are staying in her parents' home in a suburb of Berlin. The children have been here before so it is not, she hopes, too great a change for them. She has tried to create a routine for them, though things have been getting increasingly difficult with Marwan and she is not sure what she can do to help him since all he seems to want is to go back to Damascus.

—Why don't you put them in school? her mother Elena suggests. There's a very good one within walking distance of here. It'll keep them busy during the day, might make it easier for all of you.

—It's an idea, I suppose, replies Brigitte. But the school year has already started and if we're not going to be here for very long anyway, what would be the point?

Her parents have been kind enough not to ask her

how long she intends to stay or, indeed, what her plans are for the future, since it is clear she has no idea herself.

—And what about Anas? Elena asks. When is he planning to come?

—I told you he's in Beirut for work, Mother. He has an important exhibition there.

—Yes, but surely he'll come here once it's over?

Brigitte avoids her mother's eyes.

—You left without letting him know?

—Of course I did, Mother. He would never have allowed me to leave Damascus if I had.

—Even after you were injured in that blast?

There was a pause.

—He doesn't know about that, Brigitte admits. I couldn't bring myself to tell him and I don't know how much his parents have told him about it.

It had happened early in the afternoon, moments after the children arrived home from school, as Brigitte called to them to wash their hands and come to the kitchen to eat. She had been stirring something at the stove when she felt a sudden whoosh in the air and a moment of utter stillness before everything around her went into motion, splinters of glass flying through the air, the kitchen table shifting, plates and cutlery falling to the floor, her own body wobbling as she tried to hold herself steady, her heart dropping to her knees, blood rushing into her head and then the feel of it trickling down her face, mixed with sudden tears.

She was brought back to herself by the sound of Rana's screaming and ran into the living room to find her daughter standing in a corner, hands covering her ears and eyes wide open. Brigitte knelt down and wrapped her arms around the little girl until the screams calmed into whimpers before, in a panic, she began to call Marwan's name. He had finally appeared, shaking and unable to speak, moments later and Brigitte had pulled him to her and held him close.

—Are we going to die? Rana asked.

—No, of course we aren't, Brigitte reassured her. It's over now, sweetheart.

—But, *Mama*, Marwan whispered, you're bleeding. He reached up to touch her face.

—It's nothing to worry about, darling. Just a few scratches here and there.

She stood up slowly and lifted the children up with her.

—Let's go and clean ourselves up a bit. Then we'll call *Sitto* and *Jiddo* and let them know we're all right.

Brigitte had looked at her face in the bathroom mirror and flinched at the sight, but once the blood had been washed off, she decided it didn't look too bad. The cut that had caused all the bleeding was on her head and, touching it carefully with her fingers, she found it was not too deep. She felt it sting when she poured anti-septic over it, saw her features tense at the sensation and felt a sudden outrage at what had just happened.

This is not how I want to live, she told herself, not how I want my children to live, and I have to do something about it.

Her in-laws came over as soon as they could get through the security cordon that surrounded the neighbourhood after the bombing. By then, she had swept the glass off the floor and tidied up the apartment so that it looked almost as it had before. She had also made a decision about her future and that of the children which she knew she must not reveal to Anas's parents. She would have to leave as soon as possible, before Anas had a chance to return and forbid it, before anyone became aware of her plan to do so and she lost her resolve.

—You'll come and stay with us, of course, Anas's mother said after the children were in bed. It's impossible for you to stay here now.

Brigitte had felt herself bristle at this at first, before reminding herself that she needed to remain calm.

—On the contrary, she said. This area is bound to be safer than anywhere else now because it's not likely to be targeted again.

—We just think you might be more comfortable with us, her father-in-law said quietly, at least until Anas can get back and be with you. And perhaps you should see a doctor about those cuts, *habibti*. They look pretty bad.

—I'm sorry, Abou Anas, Brigitte said. I don't mean to be forceful about it but I think it's best if we stay here for now. I don't want to disrupt the children's lives too much just at the moment. I'm very grateful you came over to check on us but we will be all right, I promise.

Eventually persuading them to leave, Brigitte had immediately telephoned her parents and asked them to make the necessary arrangements and call her back. Afterwards, unable or unwilling to sleep, she busied herself with packing and preparing for their departure the next day.

Her mother's voice interrupts her reverie.

—Brigitte, sweetheart, she says. Anas needs to know his children are OK, that you're OK.

—Why should I talk to him when it's his fault we were there when it happened? Brigitte protests. If we had left when I told him we should, the children would not have had to go through such a terrible experience.

When her mother puts an arm around her shoulders, Brigitte allows herself to cry. Moments later, she wipes at her eyes with a tissue and looks up.

—I'd like to go for a walk, I think, she says. I'll be back a little later to take the children to the park.

—That sounds like a good idea, her mother says in her comforting, matter-of-fact voice.

Standing outside her parents' place, she is surprised at suddenly losing her bearings, at not knowing which way to turn, what street to take. Around her, there is the quiet buzz of the city of her birth, cars and bicycles and people and all the indications of life continuing undeterred. She notes the green of the trees that line the pavement all the way to the roundabout at the end of the street, at the greying sky and the buildings framed by it, grey too and plain, but there is comfort in this uniformity, she admits. In that moment, still and unmoving, Brigitte is the sum of all her selves, old and new; she is everywhere she has been and all the things she has hoped for. Thinking clearly at last, and despite herself, she is able to consider Anas not as an adversary but as being equally lost, and, like her, gradually breaking.

Chapter 14

Peter is not prepared for the call, is working at his desk when he receives it, when he hears a familiar voice, though he cannot quite place it.

—Peter?

—Yes, yes, I . . . Oh, Brigitte, it's you!

He shifts in his seat and takes a deep breath.

—How are you, Brigitte? How are the children? I'm at work and Anas isn't here with me . . .

—I called to speak to *you*, Peter, she says.

Peter frowns and waits for her to continue.

—How is he? she asks. How is Anas coping?

—Well, he's obviously had a bad shock. But shouldn't you be asking him that question rather than me?

—I had to do it, Peter. I had to get the children out.

She pauses.

—We understand, Brigitte, Peter rushes to say.

Hannah and I understand why you would have wanted to leave. It's the way you did it. Disappearing like that was . . . But what's more important now is that you're OK. How are the children?

—They're well. We're at my parents in Berlin.

—Yes, we thought that's where you would have gone. I'm glad to hear the children are doing well.

—If the children are fine, Peter, it's because I took them away from Damascus. I begged Anas to allow us to leave. I wanted him to come with us, but he kept refusing. No matter how bad things got, he wouldn't leave. Then that car bomb was the last straw. It was terrible.

He hears the frustration and anger in her voice.

—Were you hurt, Brigitte? Was anyone hurt? Anas said his mother told him you were all fine when he phoned.

—All the glass in the apartment shattered. I got a bit cut up but it's the children, Peter, they were absolutely terrified. I couldn't stay another moment after that and I knew if I called and told Anas that he would just come rushing over and try to persuade me not to leave.

—It must have been very difficult for you, Brigitte, but it's important now that you get in touch with Anas and let him know what's going on, allow him to talk to Marwan and Rana.

—Yes, I know. It's just . . .

—Look, Anas is at the gallery working on the exhibition. He said he'd be home later tonight. Call him on his mobile phone then. I won't tell him that I heard from you.

He hears her take a deep breath.

—Brigitte, Peter says. It won't be easy but talking to Anas is the right thing to do. I can't tell you how he might react to your call, but that's a risk you'll have to take.

*

Making his way home, Peter feels slightly uneasy, wondering if he might have made a mistake in trusting Brigitte to telephone and talk to her husband. An image of her standing in the doorway of Anas's studio in Damascus the last time Hannah and he had visited comes to him like an old black-and-white photograph: her fair hair stark against the varying shades of grey that surrounded her, the outlines of her body slightly faded too so that she seemed almost unreal, vulnerable, with Anas, standing with an arm around her shoulders, appearing more solid, growing rather than fading with the light.

If she decides not to call back as he asked her to, how will he be able to justify himself to Anas and Hannah? Surely, he continues to muse, the situation is largely out of his control and he couldn't have said more to persuade her? But had he betrayed his friend by not being more insistent?

Before he can reassure himself on this point, however, he senses what Hannah's objections to it might be. You may not be able to decide the outcome of this situation, Peter, he hears her say, but you are still required to do your part.

He eventually finds himself in Ras Beirut's main shopping district, on Hamra Street, and decides to go into a café for coffee and a sandwich.

Sitting alone at an outside table, Peter observes what is going on around him: people coming and going, cars moving in the cross street, numerous sounds filling his ears and a kind of fast-paced hum underlying everything. He recognizes the advantage in anonymity, the opportunity a city as large and busy as this provides for him to watch while remaining unnoticed. He is aware too of the speed with which he always manages to make himself comfortable in this detachment and wonders how much it still defines him as a man, how deep beneath the surface it really lies. In the eye of the tempest that is living in the Middle East, it is not so much the pace that often leaves him breathless but rather the intensity of life, the necessarily concentrated state of being that at once tosses and tames his soul. Within this turmoil – or at least with the constant threat of it – he has often felt himself lost with only Hannah as his anchor. And although he had once thought it would, work provides little comfort. He was never meant to be a bureaucrat, he tells himself. He became a physician because he wanted to work directly with those most in need. He is suddenly aware of a deep dissatisfaction rising in him, a longing to escape these thoughts, though he knows it might be impossible to do so now that they have occurred to him.

He puts the remains of his sandwich down and stands up to go.

If there is a possibility of living somewhere between the two extremes of being, of disconnection from or a sinking in reality, he finally asks himself, then where am I to find it?

*

In the morning, Peter joins Anas on the balcony overlooking the building courtyard. It is so early that quiet reigns, the breeze coming from the sea behind them tempering the air. Below, the landscaped garden is beautiful too so that the two men, sitting together in silence now, acknowledge release from what lies ahead.

—Up early, Peter says after a while.

Anas nods.

—Brigitte phoned me last night, he says.

—Oh, Peter says, feigning surprise, that's great. How is she? How are the children?

—The children are well, very well. I spoke to them too. They're at her parents in Berlin.

— Oh, so she *did* go there. What did she have to say for herself?

Anas shrugs.

—We didn't speak for very long before she put the children on.

Peter waits for him to continue.

—I'm beginning to think that it's over between us, Peter. I don't know what to do to put things right again. I'm not even sure I want to sort it out because part of me is still very angry with her.

Peter senses that his friend is feeling too hurt to listen to reason, though he is certain Anas's willingness to compromise will come in its own good time.

—But, Anas, you want your children back, don't you?

—Yes, of course. I'll just have to find a way of getting them home, that's all.

—And how do you think you're going to do that? protests Peter. Kidnap them from their mother and return them to a country at war?

—My mother was right, Anas continues, ignoring Peter's remark. I should have married someone from my own culture, someone who would have fit in better with the family. They just don't understand us, these foreigners.

Then, looking at Peter and realizing what he has just said, Anas laughs.

—I'm sorry, my friend. It doesn't apply to you.

—Why do you think that is, Anas?

—What do you mean?

—What is it that makes me belong more, makes you think of me as one of you, and excludes Brigitte?

—That's a strange question. I'm not sure what to say to that.

—I'll answer it for you, shall I?

—You sound upset.

Peter frowns.

—I came to this part of the world for the same reason Brigitte did, to be with the person I love, and, like Brigitte, I took that huge step in good faith. It's true there are times when things haven't been easy but I'm convinced I've been very lucky.

—Lucky?

—Well, for the most part, I haven't been made to feel that I have to struggle against my true self to gain acceptance. But it's only very recently that I've realized why that is.

He leans forward to emphasize his point.

—It's not just because of the kind of woman Hannah is, Anas, and because of how much we love each other. You and Brigitte have these things in your favour too. But I really believe it's been easy for me because I'm a man. For women like Brigitte, there are any number of conditions and rules they have to abide by before they're recognized as worthy of being the wives of Arab sons and mothers to their children.

Peter leans back in his chair.

—Brigitte left her home and stuck by you all these years because she cares about you and despite the rejection she faced. Can't you give her credit for that, at least?

—Of course I can, but she ultimately chose to leave me, didn't she? You would sympathize with her, of course, because you'd like to get away from here as well, just like you said the other night.

Peter feels hurt at his friend's mocking tone.

—This conversation isn't about me, Anas, he says. I'm just trying to make you understand your wife's point of view.

Peter is suddenly aware of Hannah standing in the doorway of the balcony but he does not look towards her. Anas seems flustered and unsure of himself now, the determination visible in his expression earlier fading.

—I found her in tears when I got home one night not long ago, Anas says after a pause. It took a while before I got her to tell me what had happened, but she finally admitted that Marwan had said something very hurtful to her.

Anas shakes his head.

—She had been trying to get him to do his homework and he refused, telling her she was an incompetent mother and should just go back to where she came from.

I tried to comfort her by saying that all children say

hurtful things to their parents but she insisted it was much more than that. 'I can cope with disapproval from everyone, even from you, Anas,' she said, 'but my own child thinking that way about me is just too much.'

Hannah moves to stand behind Peter and places her hands on his shoulders.

Anas looks up at them.

—What do I do now? he asks.

—You have to phone her back as soon as possible and arrange to go there, Peter says softly. People are what's important, Anas, not places.

Chapter 15

In her mother's face, in its gently sloping lines and heavy-lidded eyes, Maysoun sees elements of the past and the possibility of a more accommodating future; and if there are hints of dissatisfaction there, if life has left traces of shadow on features where light had once been, it has not managed to diminish its beauty, nor robbed it of its grace.

Like many women of her generation in Iraq, Nazha married young to a man nearly twenty years her senior and has now, in outliving him, discovered opportunity in aloneness, seen a gateway to herself that often leaves her breathless with joy, though it is enjoyment that is not felt without some degree of guilt. In this final stage of her life, the years move slowly, do not impose undue demands or rush her into decisions she has neither the desire nor the will to make. It is not that she is merely awaiting the end – she remains vital and strong – but that she is content to go through life one day at a time, with little expectation of happiness besides that which she derives from simply being, from observing and taking part only when and in the manner she chooses.

I know all this about my mother, Maysoun ponders, because understanding her state of mind is a preoccupation of mine, because for some reason I believe that grasping what motivates her may help repair the opening into the soft tissues of my own heart that has been hollowed out by heartbreak.

Her parents' marriage had not been ideal, had experienced moments when Maysoun, having grown up to become her mother's confidante, thought it might come to an end.

I want more than this, Nazha would protest, having stolen into Maysoun's room late at night to talk. Look at you, working now and with a life of your own. I never had that opportunity, Maysoun, and I want it now.

But Maysoun had never known just how she should respond to these confessions, had felt that, though she sympathized with her mother, siding with her would be a betrayal of a father whom she had always loved, and continued to love even after his death.

The unease between mother and daughter these days is not because they do not get along – Maysoun often despairs at how alike they really are – but because now that Nazha has come to Beirut at Maysoun's insistence and largely against her own will, they are at an impasse, caught in a place beyond which they cannot move forward. Their conversations go in circles, beginning in anger then relenting into reluctant recognition of one another's point of view, then moving again towards stubborn intransigence, a pattern at once familiar and exhausting and one from which neither knows how to extricate herself.

—But, Mother, you couldn't possibly have stayed a moment longer, Maysoun protests one morning over breakfast. Do you think what's happening in the north is going to stay there? The extremists are now threatening to advance on Baghdad.

—Don't be ridiculous. There's no way they'll let them get to Baghdad. Anyway, I never venture out much so it would have been perfectly safe for me to remain there.

—Who is 'they', Mother? Do you mean our corrupt government or is it Western countries that you're relying on to come and protect us, the ones who invaded and destroyed the country ten years ago?

—Don't talk to me as though I were a fool, Maysoun. I understand very well why we find ourselves in this position now. And it's not just Iraq; the whole region is on fire. You insisted I come to Beirut but how safe is it here really?

—Despite all the problems in this country, the situation can't be compared to what's going on back home.

132

You watched the news with me last night. Those the extremists don't kill are either being expelled or forced to fight with them. How can you want to go back to that?

Nazha sighs.

—Suffering is an inevitable part of living, my darling. Surely you know that.

—But, *Mama*, says Maysoun, her voice softening now, you and I are lucky because we can improve our situation if we want to and not continue to live our lives in fear.

—What are you suggesting we do exactly, Maysoun?

—I don't know. Maybe leave this part of the world altogether and live elsewhere.

A look of frustration passes over Nazha's face.

—How easy do you think it was for me to leave my home, my country, this time, at my age and after all I've been through? It's the only home I've known, Maysoun. Isn't it enough that relatives of your father's who escaped the fighting in Mosul moved into our house as soon as I left and are still living there now? How do I know they'll leave when I get back? How can I be sure I'll even have a place to go back to?

—But you're safe now, *Mama*. Isn't that what matters most?

Nazha stands up.

—You know, I'm not sure that survival is what matters most any more. Not any longer and not for me, anyway. Sometimes the price that has to be paid merely to survive is not worth it.

—But what is important for you, Mother?

—You are, of course, Nazha says. But you don't need me any more, Maysoun. You're perfectly capable of taking care of yourself and I thank God for that. I spent most of my life doing what I was expected to do, looking after you and your father. I . . . I'm not looking for new adventures, new places to go to. All I want is to be left alone in my home, my little corner of the world. That's all I'm asking for.

Maysoun looks into her mother's eyes and notes the kind of resolve there that she has not been able to find in herself. Is that what old age does, she wonders, convinces us that life lies not in the variety of outcomes we perceive for ourselves, but rather in our determination to survive the very lack of them?

Chapter 16

The road to Damascus begins in Beirut, a two-hour journey that climbs eastwards from the city's suburbs, through the towns of Aley and Sawfar and then to a highway that leads down to the Bekaa valley and on to Syria.

Peter witnesses moments of extraordinary beauty as he looks out of the car window. There is the point at which drivers make the descent either side of the mountain, to the left for the northern Metn, or right and towards the border, where the landscape on one side is green with trees and bush, villages appearing here and there on the mountainside, and on the other lie the barren lands of the *jurd*. This dry countryside, covered in snow in winter, now looks stark and dazzles in the sun as cars carefully make their way above the one-thousand-foot drop; it is impressive in the way that only seeming emptiness can impress, rock and dirt as far as the eye can see, and every now and then a herd of goats picking its way through the sparse vegetation.

Then suddenly, round a bend in the road, the patchwork basin that feeds the Lebanon comes into view: fields of wheat and corn, of green and gold and rich red earth too. This valley is home to dairy farms and vineyards, to the Roman ruins of Baalbek and the remains of an Umayyad palace in Aanjar, to nomadic tribes that pitch wide tents of animal hide on the sides of roads, in and out of which run children, barefoot and dirty, and somewhere also, to tributaries of the Al-Aasi river: fragrant waters that are born in the belly of Lebanon's highest mountains and emerge here to nourish the land before continuing northward into Syria and Turkey.

The first time Peter had come across this view, years ago when Lebanon was for him only a passing interest, he had looked upon it all with a healthy detachment, as a scene that pleased his senses but did not touch his heart. Now, as the car dips downwards and into the busy market town of Chtoura, stopping at countless army checkpoints set up to try to stop the free movement of arms and extremists, it occurs to him that in loving this country, he has also become burdened with disappointment in it, with frustration because separating its splendour from the cruelty and indifference that abounds in it is now impossible for him.

You are no longer fooled, Peter, Hannah said to him

recently, by the natural beauty of Lebanon or the effort-less warmth of its people. He thinks that she is absolutely right, that in expecting more than this country can give, he has truly become one of its people.

—It's taking a lot longer than I thought it would, Hannah says, reaching out to touch Peter's hand.

They are sitting in the back seat of a hired car and she looks less than her usual self, tired and anxious and her hair in disarray. They had rushed out of the house very soon after receiving the call once a car and driver had been arranged. Peter is still unsure what they will be able to do to help Anas, who was apparently arrested by Lebanese security forces while on his way to Damascus the day before. The man who phoned to let them know had been a passenger on the bus with Anas. 'He asked me to speak to you, said you would be able to help him,' the man had said. 'He's worried he'll be deported and won't be let back into Lebanon.'

At first, they had been too upset about Anas's sudden departure and news of his arrest to work out what to do but Hannah had had the presence of mind to ring her father and he had arranged for a friend of his, the mayor of a village near Zahle, to meet them there and help to get Anas released.

—*Baba* says this man is very well known in the area, Hannah tells Peter, and has connections with the army as well as the local militias. It's a good idea to have him with us.

They meet the mayor at a café on the main Zahle road. He is almost as tall as he is round, has a black-and-white *kaffiyeh* wrapped around his head, and a moustache that he periodically smoothes over with one hand. He greets them and begins the conversation by praising Hannah's father and their long friendship.

—Your father is an exceptional man, says Abou Mazen, and I owe him a great deal. I am glad of the opportunity to be of help.

Clearly not intimidated by the situation, the mayor shakes Peter's hand firmly and reassures them that everything will be all right.

—Tell your husband – he leans over to speak to Hannah in a loud voice – tell him we are proud to have him here. Foreigners are most welcome in our town.

—Peter understands everything you're saying, Abou Mazen. Hannah addresses the mayor by his name. He's just not very good at expressing himself in Arabic.

At this, Abou Mazen slaps Peter on the back and laughs out loud.

—That's wonderful, he says. Now let's go get your friend out of the mess he's got himself into. Tell your driver to follow me. That's my car over there.

They arrive at an army barracks and Abou Mazen instructs Hannah and Peter to wait for him outside.

—I'll let you know if I need you, he says, his expression suddenly serious. I think it's best if I take care of things because I know them here. Things will take time to sort out so don't worry if you don't see me for a while.

Peter and Hannah return to wait in the car while the driver steps out for a cigarette.

—Don't look so worried, Peter says. It's going to be all right, I'm sure.

He sees her raise a hand to her chest and take a deep breath.

—Are you all right, Hannah?

She smiles at him.

—I've probably had too much coffee today.

—Palpitations?

She nods.

—Nothing serious. I'll be fine, *hayati*. I just hope Anas is OK, that he's being treated well, that's all.

The infiltration of Islamic extremists from Syria and the subsequent search for them by Lebanese authorities have resulted in instances of discrimination against and abuse of the Syrian refugee population and Peter recognizes that Hannah is not wrong in being concerned, but he does not want her to worry further.

—I don't know why Anas took a bus to Damascus, Hannah continues. He would have been a lot better off going in a taxi.

—Not necessarily, sweetheart, Peter replies. They're stopping almost everyone these days, trying to enforce the new laws on refugees from Syria. The army has lost a lot of good men to the battle with the militants and they're being vigilant. The real question is why Anas decided to return to Damascus in the first place. He should have been on a plane to Germany instead.

Only two days earlier, Hannah and Peter had returned home to find no trace of Anas. He had tidied up the room he had been sleeping in and left with all his things.

—I just hope they won't use this arrest as an excuse to stop him coming back into the country, says Hannah.

Peter shrugs.

—Maybe what's happened will finally persuade him to go to Berlin and be with his family. Maybe he'll realize now that there's no future for any of them in Damascus.

—Who knows what he's thinking right now or what the consequences of this situation are likely to be? Hannah seems uneasy.

—Are you sure you're all right? Peter asks again.

She dismisses his concern with a gesture.

—I've been thinking, Peter, wondering really . . .

—Yes?

—You keep saying you wish you could get away from here. Are you serious about wanting to leave?

—Keep saying? I mentioned it once in anger.

—Once or twice – it doesn't really matter, does it? It's enough that the thought has actually crossed your mind. What if you decide to do what Brigitte did?

—You mean disappear like that? Peter protests. Are you insane, Hannah? I would never do that to you.

—Because you know I could never leave this country, she continues as though he hadn't spoken. I told you that from the start. It was your decision to come here to live. I didn't ask you to do it.

He wants to tell her she is wrong, that leaving her would be impossible, but all he can do is stare as she clutches once again at her chest and begins to gasp for breath. For a moment, he is unsure if what he is feeling is indignation at what she has said or shock that there might actually be some truth in it. He jumps up from his seat, stands behind hers, wraps his arms around her and stays there until she is breathing evenly again. He takes a tissue out of his pocket and wipes her eyes.

—Hush now, Peter says. You'll be fine, sweetheart. It was just a panic attack.

Moments later Abou Mazen returns to find them sitting side by side in silence.

—They've agreed to release Anas into my custody for tonight and we'll come back tomorrow to finalize the paperwork, he says.

—That's great news, Peter says. Will he be able to stay in Lebanon now?

—As long as he doesn't get deported, he should be fine. Once someone is deported under these new laws, it's very difficult for them to return.

—But did they tell you why they arrested him in the first place? Hannah asks.

—We don't have open borders between this country and Syria any more so they check all Syrians leaving Lebanon to make sure they have valid papers under the new regulations.

—Weren't Anas's documents in order?

Abou Mazen shrugs.

—It seems they weren't. Look, I'm just going to go with one of the officers to pick him up at the checkpoint.

He puts an arm around Hannah.

—We'll talk more later. I'll meet you back at the café. Have your driver take you there and tell him to return to Beirut. There's no point in keeping him on since you'll be staying at the farm for the night. We can arrange for someone else to take you back tomorrow.

He starts to walk away and then turns around again.

—And don't try to call me. They've taken my mobile away for the moment. Just be patient, OK?

They return to the café in Chtoura, order lunch and then spend what seems like hours waiting and wondering if Abou Mazen will indeed return with Anas before nightfall. In the half-light and as conversation fades into a comfortable silence, Peter looks at Hannah and smiles. She too, it seems to him, has been calmed by patience, her eyes following the movement of the canopy above them stirring lightly in the evening breeze. He reminds himself of a lesson he learned early on in his life and work in this part of the world: that acceptance and endurance are one and the same, that in passions receding lies the promise of tranquillity.

Hannah jumps up.

—It's Abou Mazen's car. She points at a vehicle coming to a stop alongside the café.

Anas steps out and walks towards them and Hannah runs to embrace him. Peter waits for her to let go before greeting his friend. To his relief, Anas looks dishevelled but otherwise all right.

—It'll take a good half-hour to get to the farm from here so let's go straight there, says Abou Mazen. I'm sure everyone's tired and needs a good meal and a rest.

On the journey, Anas, who is sitting in the front passenger seat, remains silent. Peter touches Hannah's shoulder and shakes his head when he sees her lean forward to speak. She sits back and sighs and, suddenly aware that she is weeping, he knows he loves her now more than he has ever done.

Chapter 17

He glances longingly at the big blue slide on the other side of the park, at the children careering down it, his sister among them, a big smile on her face that reflects a happiness he does not feel, and kicks at the bench his mother is sitting on so that she looks up at him with the anxiety in her eyes that has been there since the day they left home: a kind of startled nervousness that only makes him angrier every time he sees it.

—What is it Marwan? *Mama* asks him. Why don't you go and play with the other children?

—You want me to play with those babies? he says. I'm too old for slides and playgrounds.

He frowns when his mother reaches out to touch him.

—Sweetheart, come here.

He quickly moves away.

—No, he says, his voice rising. You can't make me want to be here. No matter what you do.

For an instant, he is pleased at the hurt look on her face before a now familiar feeling of confusion comes over him.

He does not understand why they have to be here. Berlin is unfamiliar, cold most days, with too big, tall buildings crowded up against each other and so many people. Even this park where his mother has insisted on coming every day since their arrival, the greenness here and the relative quiet, make him feel small.

He sighs. He longs for the skies of home and the familiar streets sheltered below, for the smells of Damascus, for its secrets revealed only to him, for the boy he is there and the future he had been promised.

Maybe, he tells himself, maybe if we were here on holiday, I would like it then.

As it is, he does not know how long they are likely to stay. But what scares him even more is that neither does *Mama*. When is she going to start behaving like a proper grown-up again? he wonders.

She beckons to him, and he realizes that she is as pretty as ever these days, long golden hair and the coloured eyes he and his sister Rana have inherited. Still, she seems less herself lately, thinner and often sad. For what seems to him the thousandth time, he wishes his father were here.

Only yesterday, he had tried to approach her about getting in touch with *Baba* again to tell him they were willing to return but she had been adamant, had shouted at him for bringing the subject up, for upsetting her and his sister unnecessarily.

—I've explained it to you so many times now, Marwan. Why is it so impossible for you to understand? Do you want to go back while the war is going on? Is that what you're thinking?

Unlike his sister, who was younger, Marwan had known about the unrest in Syria pretty much as soon as it started. His classmates had talked about it constantly, and he, at twelve years old, had understood most of what was said in news bulletins on television. But throughout that period, he had believed in his father's assurances that they would always be safe, even when eventually he found himself being wakened at night to the sound of gunfire and loud explosions, so that he would have to try to stop the trembling in his body, the dread that gripped his insides, by closing his eyes tightly and humming quietly to himself.

He had been able to keep his fear at bay until the day before they finally left. *Baba* was away in Lebanon again for work and he and his sister had just arrived home from school when they felt the whole building shake beneath their feet, heard the sound of glass shattering throughout the apartment. He put his hands over his ears as Rana began to scream; then, to his eternal shame, instead of comforting her he had run into his room and hidden under the bed. The moments that followed seemed endless. He remembers the grimy feel of tears on his face, of his nose running so that he had had to wipe it with his sweater sleeve because he was too scared to go and fetch a tissue. Eventually, when his sister's screaming finally died down, he heard his mother calling to him. The fear and urgency in her voice compelled him to crawl out of his hiding place and into the living room where he found her sitting in an armchair with her arms wrapped around his little sister, her hair matted and splattered with blood, both of them whimpering quietly.

It seemed to him that everything changed at that moment; he was certain he could no longer believe whatever he had once thought true: not his father's promises, not childhood nor joy, not home nor any claim to it. Sitting in his mother's lap next to his sister, body trembling, he had felt himself retch at the sight and smell of blood and immediately known guilt and shame because of it.

He wanders over to the edge of the park, away from the playground, and hides under the wide and drooping branches of a large tree. The thought that his mother would not find him should she come looking pleases him. Let her be scared, he thinks. Maybe she'll try to understand then how I feel.

Until now, his mother's parents had not figured too prominently in his life. And though he loves them and knows that they return that love, he does not think he knows them well enough to give them his unconditional trust. In Damascus, everything and everyone was familiar: the home he grew up in, the streets and neighbourhood he loves so well, his school and all his friends, the family whom he misses so much – *Sitto* and *Jiddo*, aunts, uncles and cousins; all the people who, in recognizing him, made him feel stronger and still more real.

There is something else too, something he would not dare talk about to his mother, especially not now. In Damascus, he was aware of occupying a unique place in the family, of enjoying the privilege of being the only son of an only son – the keeper of the family name, his grandfather had once explained. It meant not only that he was allowed more freedom than his sister but that, as he grew older, there were fewer restrictions on his movements than on those even of his mother and other older female members of the family. It was something that he had heard Brigitte and Anas argue about so that at times he had felt in himself the same divergence, the same struggle to accommodate conflicting ideas without success. Still, whatever the conflict, there was always the reassurance that it would be resolved, that the family, unbroken, would always win through.

But he is fearful that all that has been lost now, that in the rift between his mother and father, in the spaces between himself and his home, in the before and after of this war, his own life has been immeasurably altered, his future riven with uncertainty. And while having his German grandparents here helps soften the fall, Marwan knows that falling of some kind, that being thrust into the fearful unknown, has become inevitable not just for him but for his parents and sister too.

Rana comes running towards him, grabs his hand and pulls him out of his hiding place.

—Come see, come see, she squeals.

—What is it?

—I can slide down on my stomach now, really fast. Come watch.

She pulls at his arm but he stands his ground.

—Marwan, *bitte*?

He looks up to find Brigitte beside him and expects her to begin pleading with him again. Instead, she is smiling, her face open and with so much expectation in it that his heart leaps inside his chest.

—OK, I'll come, he says. Just stop pulling at my arm, Rana.

Chapter 18

Abou Mazen's home is not what Anas had expected. In the half-dark, as they step out of the car and walk through a tall metal gate into a garden with the sound of running water nearby, even as he sees only the shadowy silhouettes of a gazebo, of a trellis covered with climbing plants and further on a dwelling with a low, flat roof and wide wooden doors, he is aware of the scene's ramshackle beauty, of a healing stillness in the air that makes him want only to close his eyes and sleep.

Once inside, he turns to Abou Mazen and thanks him again.

—But you will think me rude now, Anas says quietly, because all I want to do is to go to bed.

—Surely you'll want something to eat first, replies his host.

Peter places a hand on Anas's forehead.

—You know, you might be running a temperature, he says in halting Arabic.

He reaches for Hannah's handbag and rummages inside it.

—Here are some tablets to bring that temperature down, Peter continues. They'll also help you sleep.

Abou Mazen smiles.

—If the doctor thinks you need to go to bed, then let me show you to your room right away, he says.

Anas places a hand on Peter's shoulder.

—Thank you, *habibi*, he says, and then, looking at Hannah, continues: I'll see you both in the morning.

He follows his host through a dark passage and into a small room at the end of it.

—The bathroom is next door, Abou Mazen says. There are towels in there and a bottle of drinking water. And if you feel cold, there's an extra blanket in the closet.

Anas is glad the temperature has turned cool since it will make falling asleep easier. Alone, he swallows the tablets, strips down to his underwear and gets in under the covers. He should shower but he cannot bring himself to do anything that will require too much effort, that will allow thoughts of the indignity he has endured, of his family so far away and of his own indecision to infiltrate his mind when he has spent this day just past trying to empty it of them.

There will be enough time for thinking tomorrow, he knows.

*

He wakes at dawn, to a rooster's call and the sound, distant and faint, of a muezzin in prayer. Getting quickly out of bed, he showers, puts on his dirty clothes once again and tiptoes down the passage to the main door and out into the garden where two men dressed in work clothes are already tending to the trees and plants.

The air is fragrant so that Anas, his heart inexplicably leaping, takes a deep breath before making his way to the seating area under the gazebo where a tattered sofa and several chairs covered in chintz are arranged around a wooden chest. He is surprised to find also what looks like an old carriage propped up in one corner, velvet curtains, once red, pulled back to either side of its door to reveal, as Anas looks in through its window, not seats, but bowed and dusty emptiness.

He decides to explore further and finds, raised on to a concrete platform, a swimming pool and around it pots of a variety of shapes and sizes filled with geraniums that are still in bloom. He dips his hand in the water and shivers at its iciness, yet smiles too because there is something so fresh and true about this blueness that, in the absence of sunlight, is pure, unsullied by external warmth, a colour perhaps impossible to repli-cate though the artist in him wants to try to do just that.

—I miss my studio, Anas finds himself saying out loud, and he is surprised at the sadness that suddenly engulfs him and at the tears he begins to shed.

When his son was still an infant, Anas would some-times take him to the studio and sit him in his baby chair on the table where he worked, and Marwan would watch as his father painted or sculpted, occasionally calling out for attention with a quiet grunt or an indig-nant baby screech that made Anas look up. As he met his child's eyes, to grin back at him and cluck his tongue with acknowledgement, he would feel a rush of some-thing unnamable, not just of love, which he had in abundance for both his children, but also of a kind of recognition of how far they had come together and where they were likely to go, their lives forever part-nered as father and son.

—Anas? Is that you?

He quickly wipes a hand over his eyes and looks up to find Hannah walking towards him.

—You're up early, she says. Isn't it beautiful here?

He only nods, afraid that if he tries to speak she will hear a tremor in his voice.

She slips a hand through his arm and leans against his shoulder.

—I want to look around, she says. Will you come with me?

She leads him down some stone steps to the right of the gazebo and towards a grove of olive trees, their leaves and trunks glinting silver as the sun, now making its early-morning appearance, leans into them.

—Abou Mazen told us last night that this place was farmed for the first time by his grandfather nearly eighty years ago, says Hannah. He was the son of Lebanese immigrants to Mexico who came here in the nineteen thirties, just before the war, and spent his life savings on this land and on building a home for his family.

She stops and looks around her.

—Apparently, Hannah continues, he couldn't speak Arabic when he first arrived but ended up remaining here for the rest of his life. And he made sure it was a working farm from the very beginning. There's this olive grove, a fruit orchard, a vegetable garden, a chicken coop and even a stable.

Anas smiles, looking at the trees that, in their completeness, seem settled here for life also, their unseen roots as much a part of the tableau before him as their trunks and branches are.

He imagines exactly what it must have been like so long ago, a man seeing in what would have been a barren patch of valley the green and bounty to come, a picture in his mind's eye that grew even as the vegetation did, that built itself into a home and into lives, into future generations who would hopefully love and nurture this place as he had.

He is aware of Hannah pulling at his arm, leading him all the way around the grove, through a gate and to a fenced paddock where sheep, a couple of very old-looking horses and several deer are feeding on the grass.

Hannah lets go of Anas's arm and walks over to the fence.

—Aren't they beautiful?

She reaches an arm out and almost immediately one of the horses ambles over to her, nuzzles her hand and, finding nothing there, lifts his head up and snorts with disdain.

She looks at Anas and they burst out laughing.

—Are you going to tell me what you're feeling? Hannah almost whispers this question to him a moment later. You've been so quiet.

He shrugs.

—You might feel better if you talk about it, Anas.

He likes the smell of the animals here, the musty scent of manure and grass mixed in with the whiff of damp fur and hide. He is pleased also at the spectacle of hundreds of insects buzzing through the expanding sunshine and the specks and spots suspended forever in it. But he is unsure what he can say to explain himself because it seems to him now that there is really nothing he wants to say to Hannah or anyone else.

Speaking to Brigitte had proven even more difficult than he had anticipated. Their conversation days earlier had been stilted and formal, with her not expressing regret for having taken the children away and he unwilling to take responsibility for driving her to it. But both had agreed that Marwan and Rana's welfare was what was uppermost in their minds and that he should go out there to see them before any major decisions were made.

After talking to his wife, Anas had decided to go to Damascus to check on his family without letting Hannah and Peter know since they would, he was certain, try to stop him. He would return to Beirut after a few days to apply for a visa for Germany, while Brigitte, in turn, put a request in at her end for him to be granted a visa as soon as possible.

A few days later, when the bus that carried him and a dozen or so passengers on the highway to Damascus was stopped at the checkpoint, he had not been unduly concerned. It would be another routine perusal of identity papers, he was certain, and he would soon be on his way.

The soldiers demanded they all step out of the vehicle and then subjected them to individual searches. Anas had opened the small suitcase he'd brought with him and watched as one of the soldiers tipped out its contents on to the ground. Still, he had been convinced that, having found nothing, they would be allowed to gather their belongings, board the bus and be on their way. But only those with Lebanese identity papers were released.

Two hours later and the remaining men were standing against a wall on the side of the road, having been forbidden from moving around or sitting down. When Anas had attempted to approach the soldier standing guard over them, he was told to shut up and return to the line. Relief came only when an officer arrived, had them moved to a shaded area where they could sit down and bottles of water were handed around.

It was then that Anas had had the opportunity to talk to the men being held with him, the majority of whom were casual labourers from Syria who regularly sought work in Lebanon.

They had told him that up until Islamic State extremists began to gain ground in the civil war at home, it had been relatively easy to move between the two countries. The local authorities had become suspicious of migrant workers after battles in the border town of Arsal between the Lebanese army and extremist fighters had led to the deaths of a number of soldiers and to the kidnapping of dozens of others. Four of the soldiers, like a number of Western captives being held by the same militia in Iraq, had been beheaded so far, with the threat of more to come if demands were not met.

Anas had sighed and watched as one of the men pulled a packet of cigarettes out of his pocket, took one and then handed the packet around. Surprised at himself, Anas lit up a cigarette and breathed in the smoke with relief. He had stopped smoking years before, soon after he and Brigitte were married and decided to start a family.

—You can't blame the army here for wanting to get back at those bastards, one of the labourers said after a pause in the conversation. But it's people like us who have to bear the brunt of it when all we're really trying to do is make sure our families somehow survive this mess.

—*Yallah*, another man said, shaking his head. If this is God's will for us, then there's nothing we can do.

There was a murmur of agreement in the group as Anas had looked more closely at them, at their haggard faces, their clothes faded with washing and shoes worn pathetically thin. He saw outsized hands roughened with work and bowed shoulders and it occurred to him then that although he had always prided himself on knowing of the plight of fellow countrymen and -women, he had never shared it. Their reality was exactly what he tried to depict in his work, as well as the greed and corruption of the governing classes that had led to it, the oppression of any kind of opposition, the humilia-tion in poverty and powerlessness. Yet, although he had thought himself familiar with all this, he did not really know what it was to be trapped by circumstance, to be broken by fear. He realized that in being a member of a relatively privileged minority he had been protected from the excesses and cruelty of dictatorship, had – once his work was recognized internationally – even been used by the regime in its effort to present a more civilized face to the outside world. He had instantly felt ashamed, not because these truths were new to him but because he had hidden them from himself so well for so long.

He thinks now of Fatima and her dream of being reunited with her family, how unlikely her chances are of returning to a home she will recognize or feel safe in. He wonders again if there is something he can do for her, for the infant she seems so willing to abandon, for a child made superfluous just by virtue of being born. The baby, he knows, will need valid identity papers if it is to have any hope of a secure future, and he is the only person Fatima can count on to provide them. He realizes he will have to return to Damascus and bribe officials to falsify the necessary documents, even if he has to put his own name down as the child's father. What would Brigitte's reaction be to that, he wonders?

An image comes to him of his wife rocking one of the children to sleep in infancy, of a bundle in the crook of her arm, her head bent towards it so that her golden hair, dishevelled because she has just roused herself from sleep, covers most of her face and all he can see as he lies in bed, with eyes half closed, are her lips whispering a traditional Arabic lullaby, the melody haunting, almost sorrowful, her rendition hesitant at first and then filled with love. And in that moment, he is certain Brigitte will feel the same compassion for Fatima's little girl that he has, will welcome his decision to save her from a certain fate.

—Anas?

Hannah, standing away from the fence now, is looking fixedly at him.

He smiles.

—You know, he says, I'm feeling a little tired all of a sudden. Can we sit down?

—Yes, of course. You must be hungry too. You went to bed without dinner last night. Come and sit under the gazebo and I'll go and get us some coffee and something to eat from the house.

When they get to the seating area they find that a typical Lebanese breakfast has already been laid on the old trunk in front of the sofa, yoghurt and *labneh*, plump black and green olives, a plateful of cucumbers, tomatoes and fresh mint, grape molasses covered with a layer of tahini, and loaves of what look like fresh mountain bread beside them.

—Oh, Hannah says. Oum Mazen has been busy this morning.

A young woman carrying a tray with a pot of Arabic

coffee and cups comes towards them. Behind her, Anas surmises, is Oum Mazen, looking fresh-faced and smiling.

—Good morning.

—Good morning, Oum Mazen, Hannah replies, this is our friend Anas.

The older woman puts down the tray and shakes Anas's hand.

—Welcome, she says. I hope you slept well after your ordeal.

—Thank you, yes.

—Ah, here are Abou Mazen and the doctor, Oum Mazen continues. Let's all sit down and eat.

The food is delicious in the way that fresh food eaten outdoors is bound to be. Anas helps himself to a bit of everything and, once he has finished, sweetens the cup of coffee that Oum Mazen hands him with two teaspoons of sugar and sits back in his seat to drink it.

Peter and Hannah seem relaxed and happy and, for a moment, he thinks of telling them what he knows he must now do but just as quickly dismisses the idea because he is sure they will try to dissuade him. Instead, as soon as breakfast is over and he and Abou Mazen begin to get ready to leave for the police station, he takes Peter aside to talk to him.

—Peter, I didn't get a chance yesterday to thank you and Hannah for what you did for me. I hope you know how much I love you both, how much I appreciate everything you've always done for me and for my family.

—There's no need to thank us, Anas, Peter replies. You would have done exactly the same. Just go get your papers in order and we'll wait for you here.

—That's what I wanted to talk to you about, says Anas. Please don't wait. It may be hours before it's all sorted out so you two should go ahead to Beirut without me. Abou Mazen will organize my return.

—Are you sure?

—Positive, Anas says emphatically.

He hesitates before continuing.

—I also wanted you to know that I understand now.

—Understand?

—I mean why Brigitte did what she did. I know that she was just thinking of the children and their safety, that I am the one who has been unreasonable. I . . . It gives me great comfort to know that all three of them are well and safe where they are because that is really what matters most, isn't it?

Peter smiles and Anas is suddenly struck by the gentleness in his friend's face.

—I'm glad, Peter says. Once you're back in Beirut, we can focus on getting you to Berlin as soon as possible.

Anas places his hands on Peter's shoulders.

—You have been a very valuable friend to me, he says. I hope you realize that.

Peter's eyebrows lift as if he is surprised at what Anas is saying but does not have a chance to reply because Abou Mazen interrupts their conversation.

—Let's go, Abou Mazen says in a loud voice. The sooner we get there, the sooner it will all be over and we can get back here.

—Give Hannah my love too, Anas says as he walks away.

Chapter 19

There is a hint of autumn in the air. Walking home from work in the early evening, Maysoun smells rain, successfully ignoring the lingering pall of diesel fumes from building generators that run regularly because of the electricity shortages.

The coming thunderstorm, she thinks, will relieve us of dust and drought and this too-long summer.

She looks up at the sky and smiles at the sight of dark clouds looming. If she hurries, she will get home just in time, although there is something in her that delights in the thought of being caught in the cleansing rain.

As she opens the door of the apartment and calls out to her mother, a clap of thunder makes her jump. She runs to shut the living-room windows and take in the washing she put out on the balcony that morning. She calls out to Nazha once again but gets no reply and, though not unduly worried, Maysoun wonders where her mother might have gone and whether or not she had thought to take an umbrella with her.

She takes off her shoes, goes into the kitchen to make herself a glass of lemonade and sits down at the dining-room table to check her emails. This is a good time, she thinks, to take advantage of the quiet to catch up on all the unanswered messages she has not had time to attend to at work.

It is raining hard now and Maysoun is beginning to wonder if she shouldn't go out to try and find her mother and bring her home when she notices that she has received an email from a colleague in Turkey. He writes that he has finally been able to locate Fatima's family in one of the refugee camps, that they are all alive and well and had heard of her flight to Lebanon. 'As to whether or not we can arrange for her to join them at the camp,' the colleague continues, 'I cannot be sure. The government here is adamant about keeping refugee numbers down. I will, however, do my best seeing as she's a widow and has a young child, and will let you know as soon as I've found out if there's anything we can do to help her.'

Maysoun reaches into her bag for her telephone to call Hannah and Peter and give them the good news when she hears her mother come through the door. Nazha walks in, soaked but smiling.

—*Mama*, what were you thinking going out in this weather?

Nazha sniffs.

—Hello, sweetheart. It wasn't raining when I went out.

She takes off her shoes and shakes her head hard so that Maysoun is spattered with water.

—*Mama!*

Nazha laughs.

Maysoun turns away from her computer and looks at her mother more closely.

—You're in a very good mood this evening, she says. Where exactly have you been?

Nazha sits down opposite her.

—The people living in our house in Baghdad are leaving and going to America. Isn't it great news?

Maysoun lifts her eyebrows in surprise.

—I can go home now, Nazha continues. In fact, I just went and booked my ticket, paid for it too.

She reaches into her handbag and pulls out an e-ticket and shows it to Maysoun.

—Oh, no, it's damp with the rain, she says with alarm. Quick, hand me a tissue.

—It's all right, Mother. We can print out another one if we need to.

Nazha's face clears.

—But that's not the issue here, Maysoun continues. Your going back to Baghdad wasn't contingent on those people leaving. We've talked about this often enough, *Mama*. It simply isn't safe for you to go back there now.

Maysoun watches as Nazha pushes back her chair abruptly and stands up to face her. There is something almost comical about her appearance, hair dripping, clothes soaked so that her spare frame is clearly visible through them and her feet splayed out to stop her slipping in the puddle she is making on the floor. But there is nothing funny about the look on Nazha's face.

—Maysoun, she says quietly but firmly, we have a few more days together before I leave. We can either enjoy them as we should or you can spend that time trying to argue with me about the wisdom of a decision over which I will not waver. It's your choice, my love.

She pauses for a moment, as if to make sure her daughter has understood that she means what she says.

—Now, I'm going to get out of these wet clothes, have a nice hot bath and then see about dinner, OK?

Maysoun says nothing and, while her mother makes her way gingerly to the bathroom, fetches a mop from the kitchen and tries to wipe away the trail of water Nazha has left behind, slapping the mop down hard on the floor and then pulling it slowly towards her. The swinging movement, the rhythm of it, calms her and she is surprised at no longer feeling the anger and frustration that have overshadowed these last few weeks of her mother's visit.

She leans the mop against the wall and looks out of the living-room window. There has been no easing of the rain and in the street below people move quickly on the pavement and in and out of the slow-moving traffic. She thinks of this time of year in Baghdad, of sunny days, blue skies and, at night, cooler weather infused with the scent of blossom and damp dust. She remembers how all this changed after the Gulf War, when the heat of summer began gradually to linger, stretching itself into autumn, until the seasons, like the people experiencing them, descend into confusion.

The telephone rings and Maysoun rushes to answer it.

—*Marhaba*, Maysoun, says Hannah.

—Oh, *habibti*, I was just about to call you.

—I . . . I just thought you might have heard from Anas. He said he was going to call you at some point to say thank you for all your help. I just thought he might have done, that's all.

—Anas? I thought he was staying with you.

Hannah tells her of Anas's arrest and release, of how he managed to convince her and Peter to return to Beirut, promising that he would follow when all along he had intended to make his way back to Damascus.

—Now he's not answering my calls and I'm getting worried about him. I'm not sure what I should do.

—It can be difficult to get through to Damascus sometimes, Hannah, because of the troubles. I'm sure you'll hear from him as soon—

—We should have brought him back to Beirut with us and sent him off to his family in Germany where he would have been safe, Hannah interrupts.

—Hannah. Maysoun's voice is gentle but firm. Anas is an adult and can make his own decisions. Where he goes and what he does is not your responsibility. Surely you see that?

She hears her mother step out of the bathroom and turns to see her stop for a moment to tie her towelling robe more tightly around her waist. Standing now with her back to the window, Maysoun observes Nazha without being seen – the slight bend in her shoulders, her deliberate movements and the quietness to her demeanour – so that her mother's otherness, her essential self, appears more sharp-edged, more real to her than it ever has before.

—I guess you're right, Hannah says, but I can't help worrying. What if something has happened to him?

—Let's not fear the worst, Hannah, not until we have more information.

—Anyway, Maysoun adds, I wanted to tell you that I've heard back about Fatima's family. Her parents and siblings are safe and well and living in a refugee camp in Turkey.

—Oh, Maysoun. That's wonderful.

—They've already been told that she's here and we're going to work on getting her out there to join them.

—I can't wait to let her know, Hannah says with excitement in her voice. She'll be thrilled.

—I'm not certain it can be done, Hannah. So let's not promise her anything just yet.

—I'll just tell her you're working on it, shall I? I think she'll be so relieved that they're OK she won't worry too much about whether or not she'll be able to join them. Not at first anyway.

Hannah pauses before changing the subject.

—How's your mother, Maysoun? We've been so preoccupied with Anas and his situation that we just haven't had a chance to come and see her. I feel so bad about it. We must all go out to dinner sometime soon.

—Thanks, *habibti*. She's fine, really. I can't get her to stay here much longer, though. She's decided to return to Baghdad next week.

—What? Surely it's not safe for her to go now? There was another suicide bombing there just the other day, wasn't there?

Maysoun sighs.

—When I try to dissuade her from leaving, she tells

me things aren't much better here so she might as well be in her own city and in her own home. There is something to what she says, I suppose.

—How are you coping, Maysoun? It must be so worrying for you.

A car beeps its horn in the street below and Maysoun, noticing that the rain has stopped, reaches over to open the window. A rush of fresh air comes in as she turns her attention back to the conversation.

—I keep thinking that all these conflicts haven't stopped people from getting on as best they can, if they have no choice but to stay. It's the same situation in Iraq. People do what they can to maintain some sense of normality. That's probably what keeps them sane.

For a moment, the thought that what has so far seemed to be stubbornness on Nazha's part might actually be determination crosses Maysoun's mind.

—Perhaps what we need to do is to look at the situation from our own perspective, Maysoun comments, rather than from the outside looking in.

Hannah laughs.

—Not through Western eyes, you mean? There's a lot of truth in what you're saying, *habibti*.

—Absolutely. So perhaps there is courage in what my mother and Anas have chosen to do – rather than recklessness, I mean. Perhaps that's the way we're meant to look at it.

She feels a hand on her shoulder and looks up to find Nazha smiling at her.

—Anyway, Hannah, if I do hear from Anas I'll let you know right away.

Maysoun puts the telephone down and then reaches out to hold her mother as close as she can.

Chapter 20

He takes a taxi because he's in a hurry to get there and also because, if he's lucky, it might make the chances of his being stopped again less likely. The car is an old American model, ungainly on the road but comfortable enough on the inside, and the driver, a fellow Syrian, is discreet enough not to try to strike up a conversation.

At one point, as they are getting closer to the border with Syria, they see a man and woman ahead of them standing on the side of the road, gesturing for them to stop.

Anas turns to the driver.

—You're not thinking I should stop for them, are you? the man says, taking his eyes off the road for a moment to look back at him.

—Well, they do appear to need a lift.

—They can wave down a passenger van when it comes by, the driver says. It's not a good idea to pick strangers up along this road these days. They could get us into trouble at the checkpoint ahead.

Anas glances at the couple as the car drives past them and feels a momentary shame at the disappointment in their faces.

This war is turning us into callous bastards, he thinks to himself.

Days earlier, when he went off in search of Fatima's baby, he had felt similar embarrassment: he'd found himself hesitating at one of the entrances to the Palestinian camp, as if the option of turning back, of giving up and abandoning his mission was perfectly acceptable. Perhaps, he had told himself, I am too caught up in my own troubles to really care. Perhaps that is under-standable.

Still, he had entered the camp, asked for directions and walked through a maze of bare concrete construc-tion, two- and three-storey structures stacked on top of each other with a narrow dirt path winding itself between them, vertical villages, pretences of homes. As he walked beneath ugly, swathed tangles of electrical wire that skimmed the top of his head, blocking out the light, the lack of air, the sense of being slowly stifled, threatened to overwhelm him. He had stopped and closed his eyes. When he opened them again, there was a familiar-sounding clunk coming from nearby and, looking to his left, he saw a wide doorway through the gloom and within a pool table, two boys, cue sticks in hand, playing in silence. For a moment, he stood trans-fixed, until a moped came to a sudden stop behind him, its horn tooting for him to move aside. He thought of the waves of Palestinians who had sought refuge here, first in 1948 when the Zionists attacked their towns and villages and drove them out of their homes, again when the Israelis occupied the West Bank and Gaza after the 1967 war, and now when many who were living in refugee camps in Syria had fled the fighting there. Over time, the refugees had built haphazard structures they were not permitted to own on land leased from Lebanese landlords, installed basic infrastruc-ture, opened sheds that masqueraded as shops and which catered to the refugee population, set up schools and clinics with the help of local and international non-profits, married and bore children, and lived and died waiting for the day they would be allowed to return to Palestine.

Is it possible, Anas wondered as he finally arrived at the house he had been directed to, that those fleeing the violence in Syria would suffer the same fate as the Palestinians had decades before?

A middle-aged woman opened the door and nodded when Anas introduced himself.

—Fatima phoned and told me you would be coming, she said. Come in.

She showed him into a small ground-floor sitting room crammed with heavy furniture upholstered in green velvet. There were no windows, no light and little air.

An elderly man, wrapped up in blankets, sat in one of the armchairs. He looked up at Anas's greeting but said nothing.

—Please sit down, the woman said, gesturing to the sofa.

It was only after he had agreed to drink a cup of the coffee she made on a stove in the corner of the room that she finally told him what he wanted to know.

—The baby is not here, the woman said, but I have been checking on her every day and she's doing well.

—Where is she? Anas asked, unable to avoid a note of accusation in his voice.

The woman looked uncomfortable.

—I have children of my own, you see, lots of responsibilities of my own. When Fatima said she would not be able to return for the child for a while, I put it with a family staying not far from here. They're relatives of mine, an older couple who haven't been here very long.

Anas looked around in confusion.

—But I need to see her, he said. I promised I would.

—Fatima didn't say anything about that. The woman hesitated. But I suppose I could take you round there. The children won't be home from school for a while so I have some time to spare.

—Thank you.

After checking on the old man, the woman led him out of the door and in the direction of the southern perimeter of the camp, Anas taking note as the dwellings became steadily shabbier, the alleyway still narrower and less clean and an unpleasant smell began to fill the air. When they arrived at a battered doorway, she gestured for him to step into a room empty of furniture, where the concrete floor was only half covered with straw mats, thin cushions lining one wall and barefoot, unwashed children crawled and wandered and stared at him. Before disappearing into another part of the apartment, the woman asked him to sit down and wait for her.

He looked around at the damp, peeling walls, felt himself losing hope; earlier determination left his body and seeped into the floor beneath him, and he began to wonder if he should not have taken Hannah and Peter into his confidence before coming here. As it was, he had found himself suggesting to Fatima when they spoke that he might be able to find a good family to adopt the child. What was I thinking? he asked himself. What if, in the end, I can't help and I've just built her hopes up for no reason?

The woman came out with a small bundle and handed it to him. He looked down at the baby loosely wrapped in a dirty cotton blanket, the tufts of dark hair sticking out of its head, the tiny features and delicate, flaky skin.

—She was asleep, the woman said, her loud voice startling the infant awake, but you insisted on seeing her so here she is.

The baby began to squirm, its little hands, fingers and palms drawn like paws, moving up and down with its body.

—You woke her, Anas said, feeling suddenly irritated with the woman.

He began to swing the baby gently to and fro, and watched her blink several times before she finally settled. When he looked up again, the woman was frowning at him.

—What's her name? he asked.

She sniffed loudly.

—You'll have to ask Fatima, she said. She didn't mention a name to me.

Hearing the disdain in her voice, he wanted to shout at the woman, berate her for her obvious indifference, but stopped himself.

—I don't know when the mother is planning to return, she continued, but I won't be able to look after this baby much longer. The money Fatima gave me has run out and I simply can't afford it.

—Don't worry, Anas said, realizing she was expecting some sort of payment from him. I'll help you with that but you need to take care of the baby yourself. I'm not happy with the conditions here. I'll also tell Fatima to come back for the child very soon so she won't be on your hands for much longer.

He pulled out some notes from his pocket and handed them to her.

—God keep you and yours safe from harm, *inshallah*, she said in a placating tone. I'll take her home with me right now, if you like. You're right. She'll be much better off with me.

The baby whimpered and Anas looked at her once again. What I'd really like to do, he thought, is take you away from here, turn your fate around and give you the life you deserve. He tickled her under the chin and she smiled up at him.

—I'll be back, he whispered. I'll be back soon.

He is woken from his reverie by the tooting of the car horn and realizes they have arrived at the Lebanese border crossing. They get through without incident this time, thanks to the documentation Abou Mazen helped him acquire, and Anas settles back in his seat. Soon he is looking out at the barren and dusty landscape that forms the no man's land between the two countries. From this angle, the road, wide and smooth, appears endless, and the surrounding terrain of yellow dirt and rocky hills, the starkness, reflects the emptiness he is feeling. He senses that in this brief interlude between the past and the present, he has been granted pause to reflect and an unexpected clarity of vision.

As soon as he gets to Damascus, he will telephone Brigitte and tell her he wants to make amends.

I'm sorry, he will say. I want to come to Berlin to see you and the children, to talk and sort things out. I love you.

—Sorry?

He is suddenly aware of the taxi driver addressing him.

—Did you say something?

—No. I . . . I must have been talking to myself.

—We should be there very soon, the driver continues. Glad to be home?

Anas laughs nervously.

—Yes, I suppose I am, he says. Yes, I am.

Chapter 21

Peter buys a string of flowers from an old man on a street corner, a necklace of jasmine blossoms that emit a sweet-smelling fragrance and which he places in his jacket pocket before walking slowly on.

On his way to work, across a bridge and further towards the city centre that was rebuilt after the end of the civil war, he contemplates the sights and sensations of Beirut, the subdued activity of early morning relieved by unexpected instances of beauty: the flower man raising a trembling hand in thanks as Peter turns away; the arc of outstretched arms outside a bakery kiosk; hurrying feet on uneven pavements that move in line with his own; and here and there, a fleeting impression of possibility, a glimpse of the city that once was.

He stops to cross the street and looks up at a 1920s building built in the period when Lebanon was still under French rule and the city's architecture reflected that: balconies that cut elegant curves into the near air, wooden shutters and balustrades painted in a glossy green against a quiet façade of unruffled stone.

When he first arrived in Beirut, sometime before he and Hannah married, he had lived in a building similar to this, though it had not benefited from renewal like this one has, was, in fact, in a state of undeniable decay: crumbling stairwells and paint peeling off its interior walls, the front doors to most of the apartments chipped and unsightly, and a pervading smell of damp or worse coming from the plumbing. He had tried to improve the state of the one-bedroom apartment he rented, made the best of its high ceilings and well-proportioned rooms, spent most mornings on the tiny balcony overlooking the main street drinking coffee and learning patience.

The first time Hannah visited him at the apartment, she had told him with a smile that he was turning into a true Lebanese.

—How so? he had asked, bemused.

—Well, for most of us, the world stops just outside our doorstep.

—I'm not sure I understand what you mean.

Though they knew one another well by then, he could still be surprised by some of her comments.

—During the civil war, when there was so much chaos going on around us, our homes became havens of peace, she said. Apartments were usually immaculate, their furnishings in good repair and a general air of comfort about them. Battles could be raging on just a few streets away and people would still come home after work and sit at their tables for meals, make conversation or watch television and generally get on with their lives as though being indoors was protection enough—

—Which it often wasn't, of course, he interrupted, because so many apartment buildings were hit by rockets and riddled with gunfire. Many inside them were killed.

She shook her head.

—Maintaining the illusion that one was safe inside one's own home was vital, Peter. It's what kept most people going despite the madness that was outside our control anyway.

—I guess it's impossible to be in a continuous state of fear for one's life.

—Exactly. It's not that you allow yourself to become indifferent to the violence but you tell yourself the shield you have built around yourself and those you love somehow makes you invulnerable to it.

But things are very different now, he thinks. There is no war going on but the sense of despair is evident. Perhaps also the presence of hundreds of thousands of refugees has exposed the fragility of the situation even to those Lebanese who would rather ignore it, revealed the incompetence and corruption of the country's politicians and the indifference of other Arab countries as well as the West to its plight. He stops in mid-step and takes a deep breath.

When did my days, Peter asks himself, begin with a burden of weariness that weighs me down as soon as I wake, plagues all the hours that follow and eats away at my resilience?

Hannah had told him, on their return from the Bekaa only days ago, that she sensed an unfamiliar distance in him.

—What is it, Peter? she asked.

—I'm not sure.

—Is it this whole thing with Anas?

—I suppose it's partly that. I don't know.

—Has something happened to upset you? Surely we can talk about it, whatever it might be.

He shrugged.

—Maybe I'm just tired of everything, Hannah, he finally said. I don't know.

—It feels — she hesitated for a moment — it feels almost as though you've lost faith in this country, in all of us . . .

—Don't be ridiculous, Hannah, please. Let's just stop talking about it.

But is that what has, in fact, happened? he asks himself. Do I no longer believe in Lebanon, in being here, and if so, what should I do next?

He spends the next few hours at his desk making calls and meeting in conference rooms with administrators like himself who have lost heart in the causes they once espoused. He does not telephone Hannah to ask how her day is going, does not go out for lunch, does not indulge in conversation with colleagues and feels his spirits steadily drop until, finally deciding to return home, he realizes even standing up is an effort. Perhaps, Peter thinks, I am coming down with something.

Stepping out of the office and moving towards the lifts, he stops at the reception desk to announce his departure; absently putting his hand in his jacket pocket, he finds there the wilted necklace of flowers he bought earlier in the day. He lifts it out of his pocket and leans forward, but finding no rubbish bin to throw it into, holds it up towards the receptionist.

—Oh, is that for me? the young woman asks him. I love jasmine!

He is startled by the obvious excitement in her voice, looks more closely at her and sees a pretty face, soft eyes and clear skin. He cannot now tell her, he realizes, that he had only meant for her to throw the flowers away.

—Dr Peter, how sweet, she says, her voice very soft now.

She knows my name and although I see her every day, I cannot remember hers, he thinks, feeling instantly ashamed.

—It's a bit tired now, he says nervously. I forgot it in my pocket from this morning.

She sniffs delicately at the flowers and then stretches her hand out to him.

—It still smells wonderful, though, she says. Here!

But he is only aware of the aroma of her perfume, a clean, sharp scent that is suddenly very appealing.

She is pretty, he thinks, but what is her name again?

—Are you OK, though? she continues. You're not feeling well? Is that why you're leaving early?

She giggles before continuing.

—We would really miss seeing you at the office if you fall ill. We count on you being here every day.

And then more quietly, she adds:

—I count on you being here.

He feels himself blush at the implication in this last remark.

—No, no, I'm fine. I . . . I just wanted to go out for a bit of fresh air. Would you like to come along?

As soon as he says these words, he immediately wishes he could take them back.

—Well, I'm just about due for a break, she replies, looking up at the wall clock. Can you give me a couple of minutes and I'll meet you downstairs?

He nods, feeling suddenly helpless.

—OK.

Waiting for her at the building's entrance, Peter is feeling calmer now. He has decided to take her to the café around the corner and eventually use some kind of excuse to leave. What harm could a cup of coffee do, after all? He would tell Hannah all about it later and she would agree that he had done the right thing. But he is surprised, nonetheless, at how easy it had been to charm the young woman into accepting his unintended invitation. Had she been waiting for it all along? Had he at some point given her the wrong impression?

He watches her come out of the lift, notices for the first time how tall and slim she is, and the graceful way she walks. Up close, he realizes that she has taken the opportunity to brush her hair and there is a glow to her cheeks that had not been there before. This makes him smile, despite his nervousness.

—I'm so glad, she says, that we're finally getting the opportunity to get to know one another. She reaches out and lays a hand on his arm. Where shall we go?

His telephone rings before he can answer.

—Hello?

The young woman does not look very pleased at the distraction. He mimes an apology and steps away.

—Hannah? Are you all right?

He listens for a moment and, looking at the young woman beside him, frowns and closes his eyes. At the anguish in Hannah's voice, he feels tension in his chest. What had he been thinking?

Then, walking away without looking back, he tells Hannah he will be right there.

Chapter 22

Hannah meets her father on Hamra Street and they walk slowly towards their destination. Although Beirut usually experiences four distinct seasons, the weather is hot again and as they walk, her arm holding tightly on to his so that she is lifting him slightly, he tells her of an old saying his mother used to repeat at this time of year: Between October and November is another summer.

Hannah is amused at the idea of seasons concealed behind the months that bear them, repeats the saying to herself and thinks again how much she misses being with her parents and her brother at home, of Arabic being passed along from room to room and from one day into the next, of the uncommon ease in which they lived before the civil war and the sense of safety they enjoyed in having no idea that things would soon change for them forever. She thinks also that even now, in this new and harsher Beirut where people and places have changed to accommodate the pressures they live under, there remain gentle impressions of the city's more reliable past, reminders that come to life from time to time and which provide comfort.

Faisal comes to a stop and jerks Hannah towards him as he does so.

—All right, *Baba*?

He shakes his head.

—Just taking a breather. You walk a little too fast for me.

—I'm sorry! Let me find somewhere for you to sit down.

—No, no, Hannah. I'm all right. Just give me a minute to catch my breath.

It is early afternoon and the streets are quiet before commuters begin to make their various ways home. Still, there are enough cars driving past to give the impression of movement and in the shops along the street on which they walk a few customers linger. Standing so close to her father, Hannah imagines herself part of a larger, more steadfast whole.

—OK, let's go, Faisal says moments later, and they do, past the Commodore Hotel which previously housed much of the international media covering the civil war; across Lyon Street that runs parallel to Hamra – though its traffic moves in the opposite direction – and which eventually leads to the city's central business district and further to East Beirut; down Labban Street, past a pharmacy in which Hannah remembered her mother shopping, a grocer's and numerous small shopfronts; then up stone steps towards the Hariri mansion where the country's former prime minister – assassinated some years before – and his family once lived but which now stands empty but for the security guards that man its gates; and finally to a large and ungainly building that appears to pitch forward halfway up a hill and which, surrounded on all sides by even taller structures, is forever deprived of natural light.

Hannah sees a young woman lean out of a window a few floors up and put out washing on a clothes line. How long, she wonders, will it take to dry in shadow?

—I checked with Aunt Amal before we left, she turns to tell her father. The electricity won't be cut off until later this evening so the lift is definitely working now.

—Thank goodness for that, replies Faisal.

She gently steers her father towards the front entrance and they get into the lift.

—Your aunt should have left this old place when her husband passed away, Faisal says. I told her she could move in with me but she wouldn't listen.

—I know, *Baba*. You're right, of course, but she may yet change her mind. Give her time.

—She's lucky enough to still be paying the same rent she did before the war, he continues, so she'd get a good sum in compensation for getting out.

It is so dark on the landing that Hannah uses her mobile to light their way. Amazing, she thinks, the discrepancies in Beirut now, luxury buildings alongside crumbling ones such as this one, apartments that sell for millions and others where tenants continue to pay the equivalent of only several hundred dollars a year in rent. The civil war caused the deaths of hundreds of thousands, destroyed much of the country's infrastructure and forced a huge chunk of its middle class to move abroad. Now, nearly twenty-five years after it ended, these losses have, it seems to Hannah, been merely glossed over, have been replaced with rabid construction, a generation of Lebanese with little awareness of their country's past and over a million displaced Syrians struggling to survive, living without hope.

—Careful, *Baba*, she says quietly as they arrive at her aunt's threshold.

—*Ahlan*, *ahlan*, Amal says, opening the door, one hand holding it wide and the other hanging on to her walker.

Faisal goes in first, gives his sister-in-law a peck on the cheek.

—For heaven's sake, Amal, he says. Why haven't you got any lights on? It's like walking into a cave in here.

Hannah embraces her aunt and reaches for the light switch.

—*Baba*, it's customary to ask after people when you

walk into their home, she protests, turning to the old woman. How are you, *Khalto*?

—I'm fine, *ya rouhi*. And don't worry about your father. He tells me off about something or other every time he comes over.

Faisal walks into the living room and pulls open the French doors that lead out on to a balcony where old rattan armchairs are crowded around a glass coffee table.

—Let's sit out here. He gestures to the two women. It's too stuffy inside, all that old furniture and those carpets.

Hannah lays a hand on her father's arm in the hope that he will tone down his criticism but he shakes it off.

—My daughter, he says turning to Amal with a smile, is always worried that I am too hard on you about this place. Perhaps she doesn't realize what good friends we are and how much I love coming here.

The balcony is small and the many flowerpots that line its edges serve to make it seem even smaller. Walking up to the railing, Hannah looks out at the surrounding buildings, takes in an impression of dense-ness, of immovable human proximity, and is surprised at feeling reassured instead of tested by it. She leans over a little further and looks at the adjoining verandah to the right where white plastic chairs hang on the balustrade and a dim overhead light reveals a freshly mopped floor. The apartments are so close together that she can smell the disinfectant used on the tired but gleaming tiles.

She turns around and offers to go back inside and make the coffee.

—I've put out the pot and the cups and saucers on the worktop and the coffee's in a jar in the freezer, says her aunt. Don't mind the mess. The cleaning woman is due to come tomorrow so she'll take care of it.

In the kitchen, Hannah puts the water on to boil and begins to tidy up a bit, washing the dishes in the sink, wiping down the work surfaces and giving the floor a quick sweep before making the coffee. She dare not do more for fear of upsetting her aunt and thinks, not for the first time, that she should make an effort to come here more often to help out. Amal's two daughters live overseas and come to visit only once a year so the old woman, who has so far refused to have a live-in house-keeper, is alone much of the time. It is a dilemma, Hannah realizes, that many who emigrated and left elderly parents behind have to face.

When she takes the coffee tray out to them, her father and aunt are sitting together in silence. She real-izes that although the balcony looks directly on to the street, it feels just as closed in and stuffy as the rest of the apartment.

—When did you and Khalo Nabil move in here? she asks her aunt before she sits down.

—Goodness, that was a long time ago, says Amal.

As soon as we got married, so that would be about
forty-five years ago, I think.

—The building was brand new at the time and was
considered one of the best places to live in this area,
Faisal adds. Had a lot of greenery around it, I seem to
remember?

Amal nods.

—Yes, it did. Things were very different. She points
in the direction of the villa. That was the only building
anywhere near here, and it didn't block out our view
either. Your Uncle Nabil and I were invited to a party
there once long ago.

—To the Hariri villa?

—It didn't belong to Hariri then, Amal continues. It
was owned by a Druze member of parliament, a very
wealthy man. He held a reception once and invited lots
of people from the neighbourhood.

—Probably after people's votes, Hannah says with
disgust.

—No, *habibti*, her father objects. He stood for elec-
tions in his mountain village, so constituents here
wouldn't have been able to vote for him anyway.

—But people around here did go to him for help from
time to time, Amal says. I still remember what it was
like inside those gates. A beautiful garden with fountains,
and the house was huge, marble floors and vaulted ceilings.

—It can't have been as impressive as the Daouk villa
up the road, Faisal says. I've been inside, you know.

There follows a mild argument between Faisal and Amal that Hannah does not participate in. Instead, she listens and tries to imagine her father and aunt in their youth, sitting together like this, perhaps with others looking on, with Hannah's mother and other members of the two extended families enjoying days brimming with promise. She has seen photos of them, of course, black-and-white ones that make them appear even more removed in time, taken in places that no longer exist and with people who have already passed on, ephemeral images of themselves as they dreamed goals that have long since been gained and lost.

She listens and sees all this and feels a sudden, private sadness which their obvious pleasure in being together does not dispel. Hannah is still deep in thought when her mobile rings and she answers it. Later, she will not remember the exact words that Anas's sister used to let her know of Anas's disappearance. Then as soon as she hangs up, Hannah dials Peter's number.

—Peter, *habibi*, she begins.

—Hannah? Are you all right?

She takes a deep breath.

—Anas's sister just called. It's Anas. They have no idea where he is – his family, I mean.

—I don't understand.

—It seems he never made it to his parents' place in Damascus. They weren't sure when he was meant to arrive and assumed he hadn't left Beirut yet.

She sits down abruptly and bangs the back of her head against the balustrade. The notion that she has somehow had this conversation before, that the experience is familiar, takes over as a wave of knowing apprehension threatens to overwhelm her. Could something terrible have happened to Anas? She begins to panic at the thought. Why didn't we bring him back to Beirut with us that day? Please, God, let him be all right.

She is suddenly filled with foreboding, heart racing and a tingling sensation permeating through her body, an almost unbearable heat. She squeezes her eyes shut and tries to take a breath, but is unable to do so, unable to shake off the crushing fear threatening to swallow her up. For a moment, there is nothing in the world but this dread growing inside her. For a moment, she wonders if she too might vanish.

—Hannah? Are you all right? Are you still there?

—Peter, she whispers into the telephone. Help me, please.

Her body closes in on itself and she is at once immobilized. She feels someone bend over her and she clutches at the extended arm.

Eventually, as the panic begins to ebb, she opens her eyes and realizes it is her father's arm she has been squeezing.

—What's the matter, sweetheart? Faisal asks.

She hears also Peter's voice at the other end of the line.

—Are you there, Hannah? I'll be right there.

Hannah looks up at her father as she puts her phone back into her bag.

He hands her a glass of water and she sips at it carefully.

—Has this happened to you before, *habibti*? he asks.

Hannah nods.

—Only once or twice. She tries to make her voice sound reassuring. It's nothing. And before Faisal can question her further, she continues: It's Anas, our artist friend. He left for Damascus a couple of days ago and still hasn't arrived home. He didn't even tell us he was going, and Anas's sister just found out he never actually got there.

—Terrible, Amal mutters and on hearing this Hannah understands that her worst fears about the war in Syria, that someone she knows and loves would be lost to it, may yet be realized.

Chapter 23

It is late. She sits on the balcony overlooking the building's courtyard, alternately looking up at the stars and then down at the outlines of her self, her hands shadows in her lap, her breath imperceptible even as she becomes aware of it. Behind her, where she cannot see it, is the Mediterranean Sea rising and falling against the rocky, uneven shoreline of Beirut.

She tries to recall a prayer her mother used to whisper in her ear at night, melodious words in classical Arabic that guaranteed protection against the dark and which she often repeats to herself whenever fear grips her and insight is out of reach. 'Dear one, to you I surrender myself this night and upon your shoulders I lay my burdens. You are my light, the shelter and serenity that I seek.'

The thing about grief is its lack of precision, the way it pervades one's being without discrimination, refusing to be compartmentalized, sinking in its own significance and pulling me down with it no matter how hard I pray or how long I wait for it to diminish. In Anas's death I am reliving past sorrows: Mother's passing and the missing her that followed; Lebanon's demise, the death of thousands and the loss of belonging that has gone with it; the slow but certain dissolution of the Arab world so soon after hopes for its deliverance had been high. I am aware also that the devastation I feel will inevitably lead me towards total surrender to it until I am confronted with the choice of either surviving it or disappearing completely in its shadow.

Anas was killed when the car he was travelling in stopped at a Syrian army checkpoint that was hit by mortar fire. Although there were no survivors inside the vehicle and identifying the victims would not have been possible anyway, the identity cards of the driver and his passenger were eventually found behind the barricade of sandbags where an officer had been inspecting them at the time of the explosion. It was several days before Anas's family was informed and some hours after that when Peter and I were told.

—Does Brigitte know? Hannah had asked Anas's sister when she spoke to her.

—Yes. I telephoned and told her.

—What will she do now?

There was a long pause at the other end.

—I don't know what she plans to do, came the reply. I'm so angry with Brigitte right now I don't even want to think about her. It's the children I'm most concerned about.

But Hannah thinks of little else now that the initial shock begins to attach itself to her everyday routine. As she somehow moves and breathes, she asks herself again and again what Brigitte and the children, who had been eagerly anticipating their father's visit, will now do without him. How will they ever survive this?

These are thoughts that break her heart anew every morning when she wakes up to the memory of what has happened and must will herself out of bed and get on with the day; thoughts which, again, as she gets into bed at night and tries to fall asleep nestled in Peter's embrace, chip leisurely at her soul.

When Hannah and Peter telephoned Berlin and asked to speak to Brigitte, her mother had explained in halting English that her daughter could not talk to anyone at the moment, that she needed time.

—Just tell her that we love her and are thinking of her and the children, Hannah said. Tell her also that she must let us know if there is anything at all we can do to help. Please make sure you tell her that, she pleaded.

Hannah had felt surprise at feeling somehow let down, even resentful afterwards, as though in speaking with Brigitte, in trying to comfort her, she might have had the chance to alleviate her own sorrow. An opportunity had been missed.

Peter comes out to join her, sitting in the chair opposite hers.

—Are you coming to bed? he asks.

—I'm not ready yet.

—You haven't slept well for days now, Hannah. You need to look after yourself better.

—Don't fuss, Peter, she protests. All the medical tests you made me have were fine.

—All I'm saying, he continues, frustration in his voice, is that you need to relax more.

Then, more gently: I'm concerned about you, sweetheart. I really think you should be taking something for the panic attacks.

She shakes her head.

—I'm not willing to take sedatives, Peter.

—Sometimes medications are the only answer.

—I'll try to relax, she says. I promise I will.

Then, just as he begins to get up, she remembers.

—I meant to tell you earlier, Hannah says. I got a call this afternoon from Philippe, the owner of the gallery hosting Anas's exhibition. He thinks having the opening on the scheduled date is a good idea. He seems to feel there's no sense in delaying or cancelling.

She takes a deep breath.

—Anyway, I told him we'd get in touch with Brigitte and let him know what she wants to do.

—Anas's work will be even more desirable now, I suppose, says Peter.

Hannah is surprised at this.

—As tragic as Anas's death is for those of us who loved him, he continues, his family will need the income from sales of his work. This is an opportune moment for that.

—But so soon after his death, Hannah protests. It seems indecent somehow.

Peter looks at her with great tenderness.

—Hannah, he says, maybe it's time you let go of your anger and frustration over a situation you can't control. Are you sure you're not taking this war too personally? Anas happened to be in the wrong place at the wrong time and all we can do, as close friends, is try to help his family.

—That's exactly what I want to do, she says, but somehow I can't get myself out of this dark hole.

—I lost a close friend too, he says. I'm trying to get beyond the sorrow just like you are.

She is unsettled by the disappointment in his voice and feels a familiar panic spread into her chest. This is a moment I will remember years from now, she tells herself, as the fear beats against her ribs and, finding no release there, rises further until her neck and head burn with it. There has been something niggling at her about Peter recently, something about him that is different but which she is unable to pinpoint. It is as though he is waiting for some kind of a response from her. But a response to what?

When Hannah is able to speak again, her voice is hesitant.

—I've been so wrapped up in myself that I haven't considered what you've been going through, *habibi*. I'm so sorry.

—It's OK, Peter says, his voice softening.

—You loved him as much as I did, and I haven't once asked you how you're feeling. Will you forgive me?

But this does not seem to placate him.

—Hannah, there's no question of my being willing to forgive you or not, he says vehemently. We always forgive each other no matter what, don't we?

He looks so earnest, so anxious as he asks this question that she is suddenly aware of how important her answer to it will be to both of them. In that moment, as each appeals to the other for a reply that will eliminate all doubt from their minds, she knows what she must say.

—Of course we do, *ya hayati*. Always and forever, no matter the circumstance.

She wants to say more, something to comfort him further, something grown-up like: 'We have both done things we regret, my love, but nothing will ever change the way I feel about you, the way we are together,' but she knows there is no longer a need for it.

Peter breathes long and hard.

—Getting back to what we were talking about, he says, I really believe we should be encouraging Brigitte to allow the exhibition to go ahead – for her own sake, and the children's.

—Maybe you're right.

—Besides, what better tribute is there to Anas's life and work than an exhibition that celebrates both?

He puts out his hand and, as she takes it with hers, pulls her up and holds her close to him.

—We'll get through this, Hannah, you'll see, he says.

She lifts her head and kisses him gently on the lips.

—I don't want to ever have to do without you, Peter, she says. Promise me we'll always be together?

In the interval before he replies, Hannah nestles her head more closely into his shoulder and holds her breath.

—Always, Peter says.

Chapter 24

Peter nearly stumbles over Fatima sitting on the steps that lead up to the building's entrance. Beside her is Wassim and a large plastic bag filled with what seem to be clothes. When she stands up, pulling the little boy up with her, Peter notices a bundle in her arm. He looks more closely at the tiny face peeking through the tightly wrapped blanket.

—*Marhaba*, Peter greets them in Arabic.

—I've come for news, Fatima says with a nervous smile. Your wife and Anas told me they would let me know about my parents.

—Yes, yes, of course.

Peter reaches over to ruffle the little boy's hair.

—*Kifak*, Wassim?

He waits for Fatima to mention the sleeping baby she is carrying in her arms.

—Why don't you come up? he finally asks.

He notices the look of hesitation on her face and is immediately aware of the reason behind her reluctance. She will not come upstairs to the flat with him if he is alone.

—Hannah *fil beit*, he reassures her. Hannah is home. Please come up and speak to her yourself.

—I couldn't remember what apartment you lived in, she says. I . . . the porter told me to wait here so I did.

Since his spoken Arabic is not good enough to explain further, Peter picks up the plastic bag and motions for the young woman to follow him into the building.

—Hannah, he calls out once they're upstairs.

—I'm in the kitchen, Peter.

They step into the kitchen and he sees the surprised look on Hannah's face.

—I've brought visitors with me.

—Fatima! Hannah rushes to embrace the woman, and then leans down to give Wassim a kiss. How are you, *habibi*, she asks. And who is this? she continues, looking at the baby in Fatima's arms.

—You said you'd have news for me, Fatima says, ignoring Hannah's question. You promised you'd let me know about my family.

Peter pulls out a chair from around the kitchen table and motions for Fatima to sit down.

—Yes, and we have good news for you. Hannah sits down beside her. Your family is in a camp on the

Turkish border, Fatima, and they have been told that you and Wassim are here. I wanted to go and see you and let you know, but . . . She looks up at Peter. Anyway, our friend at the Red Cross, Maysoun, she's in touch with the authorities at the refugee camp. She's trying to see if she can get permission for you to go there and join them. We're not sure how it's going to be possible, though.

Fatima hangs her head and begins to cry and Hannah wraps an arm around her shoulders.

Peter watches as Wassim inches his way closer to his mother's chair, as though afraid of anyone noticing his presence. He has remained silent throughout the interchange between the two women. The scene – Hannah and Fatima bending over each other in a gentle arc, the little boy leaning into them like an afterthought – moves him in a way he does not quite understand.

He hands Hannah a box of tissues, fetches a glass of water for the young woman and then pours a cup of orange juice for Wassim.

—Here you are. Peter bends down to give it to him but the little boy shrinks away and shakes his head. Peter places the cup on the table and moves away.

Fatima finally looks up.

—Even if you can't go there to be with them, Hannah tells her gently, at least you know your family's safe, that they all survived.

—Where's the other one? Fatima asks. The one who

came with us to the camp? Anas? I thought he lived here with you.

Hannah looks anxiously at Peter. He shakes his head.

—He's gone back to Syria, Hannah says with obvious difficulty. But we're here for you, Fatima. Don't worry. We'll take care of you. Are you going to tell us who this is? Hannah looks down at the infant but Fatima shakes her head.

—Please, you must take me to see this woman you're talking about, she pleads. I'll explain why I need to be with my own family. She'll understand, I know she will. You have to help me. I can't cope on my own any longer.

—Is it the baby, Fatima? Hannah persists. Is it yours?

Wassim, now clearly overwhelmed by what is going on, begins to sob.

—Hannah, Peter says in English, I don't think we should keep asking her questions like this, at least not in front of the little boy. Can I talk to you alone in the living room for a moment?

Hannah takes the baby from Fatima and pushes Wassim gently towards his mother.

—He needs you to comfort him, she tells her.

In the living room, Hannah looks intently at the baby.

—Do you think it's hers? she asks.

—I don't know, *habibti*, but I don't think Fatima's prepared to talk about it right now.

—Maybe if Anas were here . . .

—Why do you say that? Peter asks.

—It's just that when we brought her home last time, she was much more willing to talk to him. I had a feeling that she told him a lot more about herself than she did me.

—Yes, I do remember but it's not going to help the situation if we let her know what's happened to him.

—The baby's awake, Peter, Hannah says softly. Look.

She loosens the blanket from around the infant so that the contours of its face and its tiny hands show through. Its eyes are wide open and seem to be looking directly at him. It blinks and Peter feels his heart flutter.

—She's beautiful, isn't she?

—You've decided it's a girl?

—Looks like a girl. Her features are delicate. Just look at that little upturned nose, and those big eyes.

—I wonder what Fatima has to say about this baby. I mean, if she brought it here to see us she must have known we'd ask questions. After all, it wasn't with her the first time we saw her and I didn't see any sign of an infant when Anas and I took her back to the camp.

—I thought you said there were lots of children there anyway.

—Yes, there were, but surely if this were her baby, she would have asked about it right away, Hannah replies. Her husband's uncle and his wife certainly didn't mention it.

—She seems alarmingly indifferent to it, Peter says.

—I wonder why that is. Peter, you have more experience with babies than I do, can you tell how old it is?

—Well, it's clear this is not a newborn. I'd have to examine it more closely, of course, but I'd say this baby is around two or three months old. Anyway, he continues, trying to sound matter-of-fact, I'll bet it's going to start screaming for food any minute now. We'd better give it back to its mother.

—We don't know she is the mother, Hannah protests.

—No, you're right, we don't, but she is clearly responsible for this baby one way or another.

Fatima and Wassim come into the living room looking forlorn.

—Does the baby need to be fed? Hannah asks the young woman.

Fatima looks at her as though surprised.

—Oh, she had her bottle a couple of hours ago but I've run out of milk. She puts her hand inside the pocket of her skirt and brings out a baby bottle. Here, she says, handing it to Hannah. You have milk here, don't you?

She sounds almost flippant, Peter thinks, or is it anxiety that she is feeling?

—Tell her that regular milk won't do for the baby, he says, turning to Hannah, and ask her what formula she's been using.

Hannah lays a hand on Peter's arm and speaks directly to Fatima.

—It's OK, she says. Don't worry about the milk, Fatima. We'll get her some, and some nappies as well. I'm sure she needs those. Why don't you sit down and rest for a bit? I'll telephone the pharmacy up the street and ask them to deliver a few things.

She tries to hand the baby back to Fatima.

—In the meantime, Hannah adds, I'll go wash this bottle in the kitchen.

—No!

Both Hannah and Peter are startled by the hostility in Fatima's voice.

—I don't have time for that now, I tell you. Just take me to this woman, please.

The baby begins to whimper and Hannah responds by rocking it in her arms.

Chapter 25

She walks everywhere, across the city, from end to end of the former divisions of East and West and up and down the avenues where the grand hotels are located. She slows down to browse through weekend street markets, though she does not stop to buy, eventually making her way past swarms of people until she finds herself standing beneath the magnificent arch of the Brandenburg Gate looking upward or in Potsdamer Platz where remnants of the wall remain, covered in graffiti, a photo opportunity for the hundreds of thousands of tourists who visit every year. In the Tiergarten where, at this time of year, the trees are losing their leaves and appear stark and particularly beautiful, she takes a deep breath of clean, cool air and pauses only long enough to fix a shoelace that has come undone, to wipe perspiration off her face with the cotton handkerchief she pulls out of her jeans pocket, or to coax her flyaway hair back into a neat bun at the nape of her neck.

The trick, she knows, is to keep moving so that the conversation that is going on in her head has nowhere to go but forward, no opportunity to stop until complete exhaustion has been achieved.

These are some of the stories she tells herself: Anas is at the airport preparing to check in when a voice over the loudspeaker announces an indefinite delay of his flight; he is on a plane in mid-air when the captain informs the passengers that a fault has been detected in one of the engines and the flight will have to turn back; or although he succeeds in making his way to Berlin, they somehow miss each other at the arrivals lounge and he ends up wandering around the city for days in search of his family.

The possibility that Anas will never come back, that she will never again have the opportunity to gain his forgiveness, is too much to endure, though there is something in her that knows she will soon have to concede to grief, that she cannot avoid facing the truth of this great loss, if only for the sake of the children. For the moment, she is content to lose herself in what she is beginning to see as pilgrimages to her favourite areas of Berlin, tributes to the city in which she was born and brought up and which, once she was grown, had given her Anas.

When they first met and fell in love, these were

exactly the expeditions they set out on together, hand in hand and with Brigitte acting as guide. In English – Anas has only ever spoken rudimentary German – she recounted to him the city's history revealed as much through its landmarks as in its many scars. Then one day, as Anas described to her his admiration for the people of Berlin because, he said, they are not afraid to face the truth about their past and move on from it, something that we Arabs have never had the courage to do, she had felt such love for him that she stopped mid-step on a busy pavement to wrap her arms around him while passersby looked on with what she suspected was a mixture of amusement and annoyance.

This, Brigitte tells herself by way of consolation, is me coming full circle – although she is confused as to how she will manage to step out of the loop and where she will go from there.

The night they received the news, her mother gave her a sedative and told her to try and go to sleep.

—There's no need to wake the children and tell them about it now, Elena said. Time enough for that tomorrow.

But the tablet had only made Brigitte feel even more agitated and, unable to sleep, she had walked aimlessly around the flat in her bare feet until first light when she dressed, put on her shoes and went out for a long walk, the telephone conversation she had had with

Anas's sister repeating itself again and again in her thoughts.

When she finally got back home, she had gone into Marwan's room and lain beside him for a while, and when he woke up had told him about his father's death, though this had been a much gentler version of the truth. She had held him close, and somehow managed to tell him that everything would be all right, that sadness was a natural consequence of loss and that he should allow himself to grieve.

When Rana eventually found out what had happened, she had insisted on sleeping next to Brigitte every night. She still does so, clinging tightly to her and whimpering herself to sleep, while Marwan, who clearly feels the need to blame someone for the tragedy and has decided to settle the guilt squarely on his mother's shoulders, speaks to her only when absolutely necessary and even then does so in a voice filled with disdain.

She does not know how she could have coped without the support of her parents, who continue to look after the children during her absences without complaint and once she gets home are the stalwart rocks on which she knows she can lean.

Hannah and Peter telephone every day. She knows this not because she has spoken to them but because her parents, who answer these calls, tell her about them. At first, she is furious when her mother says that in wanting to pay their condolences, her friends are also seeking comfort for their own grief. They loved him too, Elena tells her quietly, their loss deserves recognition and only you can give them that, Brigitte. Then, once on her own, she realizes that her mother is right, though she still feels unable to play the part required of her.

When Elena tells her that Hannah needs to talk to her urgently about Anas's upcoming exhibition, Brigitte is angered again.

—The exhibition, she cries. Who's thinking of the damned exhibition now?

For the first time, Elena tells her off.

—Don't raise your voice to me, Brigitte. Your loss does not mean you can treat me with disrespect. And don't forget, I am only the messenger in all this.

—I'm not ready yet, Brigitte continues to say until the morning her mother stops her on her way out of the door, sits her down and tells her firmly that not being ready is no longer an option.

—Your father and I will never stop supporting you and your children, Brigitte, but the time has come for you to face circumstances. There is no escaping what has happened, my darling girl. Your husband has been killed in the most dreadful way, but you have a son and a daughter who depend on you to do the right thing next. So what will it be?

It is as if, with that question, she is finally given the

opportunity she needed to break down. She falls into her mother's arms and cries for what seems like hours, hears her father call out to the children and take them to the park to play, listens to the sound of her own sobbing over the noise of traffic below, to a telephone ringing unanswered, to her mother's soft voice whispering, 'There, there,' into her ear.

In her mind's eye, she reviews her life in Damascus, considers the warmth and the frustration, the richness and at times the absence of reason. She trembles at the thought of war and marvels at the extremity of her fear. She had not been wrong in seeking safety for her children, she realizes that now, though there may have been a better way to deal with the consequences of her actions. For a moment too she sees her husband's beloved face and traces his features with the tips of her fingers for the last time, and says goodbye in a whisper that only he can hear. She weeps until she can weep no more, then straightens up, wipes her hands over her face and decides she is finally done with sorrow.

—You're right, Mother, Brigitte tells Elena. I'm willing to accept the truth. You don't need to worry any longer. I know exactly what I have to do.

*

It is as if the shape of the world itself has changed, as if, in those places where there once was something solid to lean against, there is now emptiness, gaps where his father had been that threaten to fill with uncertainty and make him falter.

In the first few moments after hearing the news, Marwan had felt himself engulfed by terror, had closed his eyes as it swept over him, his skin burning and insides on fire, until he thought that he too might be extinguished, that like Anas he too would be suddenly, inexplicably, consumed by darkness. When Brigitte finally wrapped her arms around him, he had endured the embrace as a kind of confirmation of his existence, a redefinition of the physical boundaries of his being, and had felt instantaneous relief and shame at the thought.

—Rana, she mustn't know, he had heard himself saying.

Grasping him by the arms, pulling him away from her, Brigitte had looked at him and frowned.

—Just don't tell her, OK, he pleaded. Not yet, please, *Mama*.

She nodded.

—All right, she whispered. I won't yet. Not until you're ready.

For a while, whenever grief threatened to approach and turn his life upside down, he had willed himself away from it; he had rushed to play with his sister and bask in the comfort of not knowing that surrounded her, believing himself, at least temporarily, untainted by the truth. For a while also he thought hard about his father, as if in doing so he might conjure him back into existence, fashion him out of the thin air they all continued to breathe. He recalled conversations they'd had, the details of them, the way Anas had lifted his hand to his mouth to stifle a cough as he spoke, the anticipation with which he, Marwan, had willed him to continue. He remembered his father demonstrating love for home, not only with words but in the stretch of his arm towards the expanse of sea before them during holidays at the beach, in the silence he maintained as he worked, painting the colours of Syria, the people and places he cherished, the quality of light awarded them by the sun overhead and its fleeting invisibility in moments of shade. He realized that what he had learned from his father was vast and limitless, yet filled exactly this moment, this experience of growing up into someone not only older but somehow more pliable. It was a lesson in how to be an exemplary son, one that caused him anguish now because he had been something less than that while Anas was alive.

The moment had finally come when there had been nothing else to do but to accept that the worst had indeed happened: when he watched as Rana wept and allowed their mother to hold her close; when, with a spare arm, Brigitte had reached for him too and he had suddenly realized that in attempting to assuage her children's anguish, she was also trying to ease her own. He had hated her more than ever then.

—It's all your fault, he had said, pulling himself away. It's because of you we'll never see *Baba* again.

His remark had made Rana sob even more loudly and Brigitte, looking at him, had surprised him with her reply.

—You're right, *habibi*. I thought I was doing what was best for you by taking you away but perhaps I was wrong. I shall never be able to forgive myself for that.

There was resignation in her face, defeat where he had once seen defiance, and he had realized at that moment that it would always be this way between them, that she would continue to be the parent who could not understand him no matter how hard she tried and that he would always resent her for this.

—I will not stay here any longer, he had said, his voice shaking a little. You can't make me. I want to go back home.

He speaks only when spoken to and cries when he is alone, in his bed late at night when everyone is asleep or as he walks to and from the shops on errands, his cap placed low over his forehead, his contorting face hidden from view.

It is on these walks that he begins to see a figure resembling his father in odd places, by the lift door as he is walking out of it, or standing near the kiosk where he buys his grandfather's newspaper every morning, even sitting on a bench at the playground watching over Marwan and his sister as they play.

Anas is not ghostlike, is neither solid nor transparent, though he is always silent during these sightings. He looks at no one in particular but is so definitely there that whenever Marwan walks past him, a whooshing sound fills his ears, the awareness of another's presence sending a tingling feeling through his body, troubling him. Once, strolling with his mother down the street, he sees his father walking in the same direction a few steps ahead of them. When the figure stops suddenly, the face in profile now so that he notes the unmistakable bend of his father's forehead, the straight nose, his lips pursed as they always were when he was deep in concentration, Marwan tries to steer his mother clear; but she is preoccupied with her thoughts and ignores his hand on her elbow. When she walks straight through the figure, Marwan gasps involuntarily, then watches her stop, her eyes wide open.

—What was that? she asks him.

—What was what?

She looks at him and frowns.

—I'm not sure exactly. I . . . I thought I felt something.

She passes her hand over her face and he notices

tiny drops of perspiration forming just above her upper lip. His own heart thumps inside his chest.

Had Anas felt it too? Marwan wonders.

On the day his mother sits him down and explains that she will be going to Beirut, he feels rising hope.

—I'm going with you. I want to be there for the opening. Rana too. We should all be there.

Brigitte sighs.

—I'm not sure the exhibition will be going ahead, Marwan. I haven't made up my mind about that yet.

—But it has to, he protests. It will be *Baba*'s last exhibition. Don't you see that? Don't you understand anything at all? And who said it was up to you to decide, anyway?

He watches as a look of uncertainty passes briefly over his mother's face.

She grabs his arm and looks into his eyes.

—Don't do that, Brigitte says. Please don't, Marwan. I know you're angry and upset but you are not to speak to me like that. Do you think you're the only one grieving? Is this how you treat me when I need you most? Is this how it's going to be between us from now on?

Her eyes, he sees, are hollow with sadness.

She lets go of him, leaving soft indentations in his skin from her touch, and he senses a distance between them that frightens him.

—I'm sorry, *Mama*, he says. I'm so sorry.

He runs to hug her and, in that instant, senses a shift inside him, what he had once thought true pushed aside to make way for something new, something like forgiveness.

Chapter 26

Maysoun places stacks of documents on to the shelves behind her desk to be filed away tomorrow. It has been a busy day, during which she has thought a great deal about Anas as she reviewed applications for a programme designed for the many Iraqi and Syrian artists who have fled to Lebanon. It is a project that is dear to her heart since it offers those whose applications are successful three-month residences at an artist colony in Denmark, after which the few whose work is deemed exemplary and of international standard will be allowed to remain and acquire a European passport.

She picks up off her desk a statuette that was given to her by one of the men who came in that morning, despite her protestations that she could not keep it. It is a representation of a dove in clay, one in a series the sculptor had explained, with its neck extended forward, wings closed and hollowness where its back should have been. She looks at it closely, runs her hands over it and realizes she does not like works so heavy with symbolism; she admires art that is beautiful for its own sake more. Still, given the negative experiences so many of these artists have gone through, she thinks, is it any wonder that they seek to depict suffering in their work?

She places the sculpture in her handbag, pulls on her cardigan and had just got up when there is a knock at her door.

—Maysoun, you're still here. Peter smiles at her. Typical of me to turn up just when you're about to leave.

She smiles back, and then leans over to one side to see who is standing behind him. —Come in, Peter. Come in.

He makes way for the young woman and little boy accompanying him. Maysoun realizes there is something vaguely familiar about the woman, who is veiled and dressed in clothes that are far too big for her. She is clearly a refugee, the little boy too; he has the anxiety she has become accustomed to seeing in others on his little face.

—This is Fatima, says Peter, and that is Wassim. Do you remember, Maysoun, I asked you to look into the whereabouts of her family not long ago?

—Yes, of course. Fatima knows that her parents and siblings are in Turkey?

Peter nods.

Maysoun turns to Fatima and speaks in Arabic.

—We're still working on getting you to join your family in Turkey, Fatima. I'm hoping to be given an answer soon. These situations are very complicated and it can take time to resolve them.

—But it's impossible for me to wait any longer, Fatima says, urgency in her voice. Please, you have to help me.

—What's the matter, Fatima? What are you afraid of?

Fatima shakes her head impatiently.

—Look, I just want to go back to my family. Why can't you understand that?

Maysoun looks at Peter, realizing that any attempt at reasoning with Fatima will not succeed.

She turns once again to Fatima.

—I'm going to call someone and make further enquiries about your case, try to find out what's happening. Would you like to wait outside?

She shows Fatima to the office's waiting area where there are also toys for Wassim to play with.

—Let me make that call and find out once and for all what the situation is, she tells Peter when she gets back.

—I'm really sorry to be lumbering you with this, Maysoun.

—Not to worry. The poor woman is clearly afraid

and wants to get away. Has anything happened to make her so anxious, do you think?

—I'm not sure, Peter replies. She turned up at our place with the boy and also with an infant, a baby girl. She won't even tell us whether or not it's hers. We had to stop asking because she got so agitated.

—A baby? No wonder she's so upset. Thousands of babies have been born among the Syrian refugee population in Lebanon alone, so many of them out of wedlock. If, as you told me, her husband has been dead for a few years, of course she's afraid she'll be found out. I wonder who the father is?

—She's living with an uncle and all his family. Surely they would know if she had been pregnant and had a child?

—Not necessarily. She may have kept it secret and then given it to someone after its birth until she could figure out what to do. She may have been raped or had an affair. Either way, she will be blamed for it. She thinks she's brought shame to her family and cannot possibly take the baby back with her as her own.

—On the other hand, the child may not be hers, Maysoun continues after a pause. It's always useful to have a baby in your arms when you're on the street begging for money. You get more sympathy that way. She may have borrowed it for the day.

—I can't really see her doing anything like that, Peter says, but I guess you never know.

—Surely you come across this sort of thing in your own work too, Peter?

—The truth is I spend a lot more time shuffling papers around on my desk than I do in the field. I'm very rarely in direct contact with patients, it's incredibly frustrating.

Maysoun shakes her head.

—Your talents as a physician shouldn't be wasted on bureaucracy, Peter. But I've told you this before.

—Well, I'm finally going to do something about it.

—Oh?

—I've applied for a position with Médecins Sans Frontières. If I get it, I'll be working in their clinics in the Bekaa.

—I'm so glad, Peter. That's wonderful news.

He laughs.

—I haven't got it yet, Maysoun.

—I'll keep my fingers crossed for you then. OK, let me make that call now.

It takes close to an hour for Maysoun to get the information they need.

—I've been told that if Fatima turns up at the refugee camp where her family is, she explains to Peter, then the authorities will be hard put to refuse her entry since she is a widow with two young children.

—That's good news.

—Well, not necessarily. The problem will be actually to get her there. It would take ages to organize the requisite papers for her to fly into Turkey, if we can do that at all, and the only way by land is through Syria.

Peter frowns.

—There must be a way to get them out, he says.

—There might be a solution, Peter. I've been playing around with an idea in my head, to do with getting Fatima to her family without the hassles of officialdom.

—What idea is that?

—It could be risky, though, and that worries me much more than the thought that it's not entirely above board.

—Given the circumstances, I don't think we should worry about the authorities and their approval, Peter says with a wry smile. What were you thinking?

—Well, we send ambulances into Syria on a regular basis, to carry supplies and pick up and transport patients to this country if needed, Maysoun begins. There's a route northwards from here that runs along Syria's coastline. It's long but relatively safe and we haven't had a problem using it so far.

She leans towards Peter and lowers her voice.

—The ambulance drivers have been known to ignore the presence of stowaways in the back of their vehicles. They're brave and take pride in being able to help the refugees as much as they can.

Peter's eyes light up.

—Brilliant, he exclaims.

—Let's bring Fatima in here and ask her what she thinks.

Maysoun is not surprised when the young woman readily agrees to the arrangement.

—It might be risky, Maysoun warns her.

—It's not going to be any worse than what I've been through so far, Fatima says. Wassim and I will still be refugees but at least we'll be with my family, where we belong. Just tell me what I have to do.

—Peter tells me you have a baby girl too. She could be a problem if she makes too much noise at a checkpoint and arouses suspicion.

—She won't be coming with us, Fatima says, her voice almost a whisper. Just tell me what I need to do. Please.

Maysoun looks at Peter as if to confirm her earlier suspicions.

—The ambulances set out early in the morning, she continues, before daybreak, from the car park just behind this building. When the time comes, I'll tell the driver you'll be there and he'll take care of you.

Maysoun turns to Peter.

—I'll have to see when the next ambulance is going and will let you know. You'll have to make sure she gets there on time on the day. It's within walking distance of your place, so it shouldn't be a problem.

He embraces her and leaves, Fatima and Wassim trailing behind him.

Chapter 27

The baby is asleep. After inexpertly changing and then feeding her, Hannah places a clean towel on the living-room sofa and puts her down on it, patting her gently on the tummy, humming quietly too until she finally falls asleep. She leans forward and looks at the infant more closely, the tiny nose and rosebud mouth, the dark, fine hair combed to one side to reveal a large, ungainly head, the small body wrapped tightly in a cotton blanket that is no longer as white as it should be, moving as its nameless owner inhales the short, urgent breaths of life.

Hannah is moved almost to tears by so much help-lessness and vulnerability, and wonders if this is the kind of unease that always comes with taking care of a child, especially one so young.

In the early years of her marriage, she had twice fallen pregnant and miscarried within the first few months on both occasions. By the time doctors discovered a medical condition that meant she would never be able to carry a baby to full term, both she and Peter had decided that being together was enough, that in their closeness was the kind of connection that would not be destabilized even in the absence of a child. Yet despite Peter's reassurances that their relationship was sufficient unto itself, despite the safety she felt within it, somewhere in the back of her mind doubts lingered, disappointment waited to pounce. Eventually, even these yearnings left her, and in their place, in that hollowness that love for a child would have filled, were her own pursuits, the work involved in self-discovery and in relationships.

She lifts her head and sighs. When she gets up off the couch, the child stirs and then thankfully settles down to sleep once again. She could do with a proper bath, Hannah thinks, and fresh clothes. Rummaging earlier through Fatima's plastic bag, she had found only a less than clean bottle and two cloth nappies but nothing in the way of clothing for the baby. She decides to go out later in the day and pick up some things for both children, perhaps even for Fatima too, if she allows her to do it. The weather will be changing soon and they will need warmer things to wear. She tells herself that she must also remember to ask Peter, when he examines the child later, what vaccinations she will need, whether he thinks she is receiving adequate nourishment and so on. But I am getting ahead of myself, Hannah reminds herself in an attempt to stop her mind racing.

In truth, what she is more concerned about is Fatima's apparent indifference to this child, something she finds much more alarming than anger or resentment would have been. She is filled with dismay at the idea that the baby may not yet have been given a name, and hopes that it is only anxiety causing Fatima to forget to mention what the baby is called.

She remembers once, in a restaurant in a seaside resort, observing a young mother with a child slightly older than this who came in and placed her baby on a chair beside her with total lack of interest, as though the child were a bag or something else inanimate, and not once, throughout her meal, turned to look or speak to it. Hannah, by then a teenager, had gathered the courage to go to the woman's table and bend down to smile at the child, who grinned back with such readiness and joy that she had felt vindicated for her forwardness, although even then the mother had not acknowledged the gesture.

But the circumstances of an affluent member of the middle class and those that Fatima is facing now can hardly be compared and Hannah wonders again what the reasons behind the young woman's obvious coldness towards the child really are. Is it because the baby is a girl and, like most female children in conservative, rural communities, seen as more of a burden than a blessing? The thought crosses her mind that if Fatima is determined to ignore the baby's existence, then perhaps she and Peter could take her on and give her the love and attention she needs. But as quickly as the thought appears, Hannah dismisses it, telling herself it is too late, that given the uncertainties she and Peter are facing about their future, a child would not gain the security it needed, indeed it might suffer along with them the consequences of these turbulent times.

I go out on to the balcony and look down at the garden below, quiet now at the end of the day, empty and somewhat bleak. It occurs to me now that I was harsh at times in judging my parents, accusing them of being the reason behind this or that fault in my character, sometimes voicing dissatisfaction and expecting to find reward in their apologies. Mother often said that while she was convinced having children was the best thing she had ever done, it was also the most difficult, a challenge she was not always capable of meeting and which invariably revealed weaknesses in both her character and spirit. Yet despite the blunders my parents inevitably made, there was never a time when I did not feel completely and abundantly loved. Perhaps there is so much room for making mistakes in bringing up a child that this is why Peter and I, as we grow older, feel less and less able to take on the challenge.

Chapter 28

Late afternoon and Beirut airport is not as busy as she had expected it to be. She pushes the trolley through the sliding doors that lead into the arrivals lounge and, feeling momentary regret that there is no one there to meet her, makes her way to the taxi stand outside.

It is raining but the weather is not especially cold and her thick jacket feels suddenly oppressive. She motions to the driver of a large, black Mercedes parked right by the exit, gives him her suitcase to put in the boot and, getting into the back seat, takes off her coat. The air is musty and smells strongly of cigarette smoke, something she realizes she is no longer used to and which irritates her a little.

When the driver asks about her destination, she replies in flawless Arabic and smiles when she sees the surprised look on his face. I may look like a foreigner, she wants to tell him, but I know exactly where I am going and how much the fare should be and I've also been here often enough to know my way around. She says nothing, though. Her determination to fit in must begin here and now, but it is not strangers like this one that she is trying to convince.

She pulls the window down slightly and feels rain on her face as the driver speeds up and manoeuvres the car on to the highway. Moving her head from side to side to try and release the crick in her neck, she grimaces at the sight of the southern suburbs to her right, the tall, ungainly buildings, some still under construction, that crowd up against each other and deface the skyline and the once-clear views of the mountains to the east. To the left is the green and murky sea. It is clouded because of the stormy weather, but also because of the waste water that is allowed to flow relentlessly into it and which emits a foul smell into the air. She quickly shuts the window.

Moments later, she directs the driver to take the exit that leads to the coastal road into Ras Beirut, past the Raouche Rock and down on to the Corniche, scenic spots that she remembers well and which once appealed to her, past the enormous residential buildings and hotels that block light and sea views from the more modest structures that are situated behind them. Traffic is much heavier here, cars only reluctantly stopping at lights or, worse still, ignoring them altogether, horns blaring with impatience. She sighs and sits back in her seat.

This has always seemed to her a city of contrasts that somehow manage to complement each other, a city which, though not certain of its place in the world, continues to claim it anyway, in the hope perhaps that it will one day deserve the status it wants for itself.

The last time she had been here was just over three years ago, on a weekend visit with Anas that had stretched into several days because they could not bring themselves to leave, there was so much they longed to do. They had stayed with Peter and Hannah, spent their days wandering the streets of Ras Beirut at first and then going on impromptu trips to the mountains or down south as far as Bab Fatima on the border with Israel. They attended gallery openings, went to the theatre and ate the kind of food usually found in fancy restaurants in Europe. But even then, even as she experienced the privileges that Beirut offered, she had sensed the beginnings of its demise, noticed tell-tale signs that Beirut's legendary charm was unravelling to reveal a city in anguish.

On their last night, they had sat with their hosts around a dining-room table that was weighted with food and drink and talked into the early hours with excitement about the uprisings in the region, of their implications, and with caution about the future, the potential obstacles that could arise in this seemingly unstoppable drive for justice and equality, for the end to dictatorship.

Anas, she recalls, had been the most optimistic of the four, had believed the Arab people would make the transition from revolution to nation-building successfully. But so many people are dying, she had protested. Surely there is an opportunity to do things differently here as well?

When she then voiced her misgivings that extremism might find in the upheaval in the Middle East an opportunity to take hold, Anas had dismissed her argument. That is the problem with thinking like a foreigner, he had said, gesturing with one hand so that she felt her heart sting. You cannot see beyond your age-old prejudices about the Arab world, about Islam and what you believe is our inferiority. It's pure racism.

She had told herself at that moment that she would never give him occasion to make her feel that way again, though looking back now she realizes she had failed dismally at this also.

As absurd as she knows it to be, there is a part of her that believes that in dying the way he did, Anas had had the last word, had demonstrated, to her especially, how he had always been willing to make the ultimate sacrifice for what he believed in. We are, she thinks, often cruellest to those we love most.

When the taxi finally comes to a stop, the driver wheels her bag into the lobby of a suite hotel in the Hamra district that is only a few minutes' walk from Hannah and Peter's apartment and which, when she is on her own, is close enough to shops and restaurants and general activity to lose herself in should she need to.

Her room is spacious though a bit dim, has a tiny kitchenette at one end and a clean bathroom with, thankfully, a good-sized bath. She pulls open the window and looks out at the quiet street below, at the residential buildings opposite and the shops beneath them, closed at this time of night. She suddenly experiences an intense need for sleep, for temporary oblivion.

Turning back into her room again, she unpacks, undresses in the fading light and gets into bed. There is something thrilling about being alone like this. Until the moment I pick up that telephone, she tells herself, no one who matters knows where I am, what I am doing. She sees how easy it would be to simply disappear, to leave one life behind and start another without past burdens, the weight of what has happened before.

She dials for an outside line and makes the first call.

—Brigitte! The voice at the other end sounds surprised. Is that you?

—Hello, Peter, she says after a pause Yes, it's me. I've finally made it to Beirut.

Chapter 29

—Did she mention the baby's name to you? Hannah whispers to Peter.

It is almost midnight and they are preparing for bed. Fatima and the children are already asleep in the guest room.

Peter shakes his head.

—Why didn't you just ask her about it? he asks.

—I did at one point but she completely ignored me. Then when I asked her a second time, while we were making up the beds, I still didn't get an answer. How could that poor child not have a name?

—You're really upset about it, aren't you?

—Of course I am, Peter. I was thinking about it the whole time you and Fatima were at Maysoun's. If you don't give someone a name, it's as if you're denying them an identity. It's just not right.

—You have a point there, I guess.

—We don't even know if the baby's hers, Hannah continues. She won't acknowledge even that.

—Maybe she doesn't want to admit it to herself, Peter says. Maybe she thinks that once she acknowledges the baby's presence she'll have to do something about it.

—What does Maysoun think?

Peter sits down on the bed.

—Well, she says there are any number of explanations, some of them too upsetting to think about, but the most likely one is that Fatima is the mother.

—What sort of explanations?

—That she may have found the baby abandoned in the camp and taken her on because there was no one else to do it, or more likely that she had an affair or was raped and had no choice but to have the baby once she got pregnant.

Hannah shakes her head.

—I'm sure it's hers, she says. I can't imagine her taking on responsibility for someone else's child when she already has so much to cope with. I guess she must have had it in secret. It would have been about a month before we met her. But who was taking care of it for all that time?

Peter shrugs.

—Whether it's her baby or not doesn't really matter since she's here with it now, he says. At least she didn't try to get rid of it and dump it somewhere.

—Oh, Peter!

—It has been known to happen, Hannah. Fatima cared enough about that child not to do something like that.

—I guess you're right, Hannah says after a pause. Maybe I'm being too harsh on her. Maybe once she's had a chance to rest here for a bit, her attitude towards the baby will change.

—Actually, I would have thought she'd be even more anxious not to keep the baby now that she knows she's leaving, Peter says.

—What do you mean?

—If the baby is hers, her parents aren't going to be happy about it. You know that in a situation like this and in this kind of conservative community, there's no place for either the woman or her child. It brings shame on everyone so that even if they wanted to, they wouldn't be able to accept her back into the family.

—They'll shun her, Hannah says quietly and half to herself.

—Or they'll do something worse still than that, Peter adds.

Hannah lifts a hand to her mouth.

—What are we going to do, Peter?

—I don't know, *habibti*. I don't know that there's anything we can do at this stage.

—But we have to help her somehow, Hannah insists. We can't let something terrible happen to her or the baby. You must come across this sort of thing in your work, Peter. Surely you know of some organization that would be prepared to help.

Peter clears his throat.

—Would you be prepared to take the child, Hannah, and raise her as our own?

She raises her eyebrows.

—The thought did occur to me earlier but could we really take on such a huge responsibility at this stage in our lives? Even if we wanted to, I'll bet this child is not only without a name but without identity papers as well. Officially it doesn't even exist so how could we adopt it?

—There are ways, you know, Peter says. People do it here all the time.

She nods.

—I really don't know what we can do to save this baby, but we have to find a solution before Fatima leaves.

Peter places a hand on her shoulder and pulls her towards him.

—Hannah, he says gently, you're worrying about something that we really have no control over. I'm not being callous but this baby is not our responsibility. There are thousands more like her who will never acquire an identity or a home. It's a never-ending battle trying to deal with the consequences of these insane sectarian wars.

—But I'm not trying to save thousands, Peter. I'm

talking about this one baby, this one child we could help. And what about Fatima? Could we live with ourselves if she went back to her family and they did something to her because of the baby?

Peter sighs.

—You're right, I suppose. Look, I'm too tired to think clearly about this right now. Let's talk about it tomorrow.

Hannah feels her frustration mounting.

—And on top of everything else, I have all this work to do for the article, she says. I think I'd better ring and tell them I can't do it. It's all just too much.

A familiar feeling descends on her: first the thought that this conversation is being repeated — the details surrounding it, the lateness of the hour and the quiet hum of the building's generator in the background are recognizable; then the sense of being swallowed up by fear. She gasps, clutches at her chest and squeezes her eyes shut.

—Hannah? Are you having another attack?

But she is unable to respond. She feels Peter's arms wrap themselves around her and though this does not allay her terror entirely, she is conscious of impending relief.

—This can't go on, sweetheart, he whispers in her ear. We've got to do something about this anxiety, Hannah.

She allows him to lower her on to the bed, and for a long time he does not let go.

—Is it over now? he asks.

She nods.

—You must start taking medication or these attacks will just get worse with time, Hannah. Do you want to go on like this?

—I couldn't bear that, she says.

He rocks her gently back and forth and she begins to weep, muttering, 'Oh, oh,' between sobs.

*

Waking to the dark, she tosses and turns, listens for Peter's deep breathing and is still awake sometime later when she hears the baby whimper. She gets out of bed and tiptoes into the spare room. In the moonlight coming through the window, she sees the shapes made by Fatima and Wassim on the mattress, two gently curved Cs nestling into each other. She steps closer, notices movement at the foot of the mattress and bends down to look. When she picks up the baby she realizes that both her nappy and blanket are wet. She makes her way carefully into the kitchen, turns on the light above the stove and looks down at the bundle in her arms. The baby is staring up at Hannah and smiling, her tiny body almost completely still, her eyes unblinking.

—Not one to complain much, are you, sweetheart? Hannah says softly. She bends down and plants a kiss on the baby's forehead. Little angel, she whispers.

As I write, I admit to having been accused, by my American husband recently and by editors on a few occasions in the past, of taking the stories I cover too much to heart, of allowing my emotions to taint my supposed objectivity and making of issues meant to enlighten the general public something akin to personal.

I have tried to justify my position as the inevitable consequence of writing human-interest features which have to contain a measure of humanity in them to be interesting, but I concede the point also, the assertion that in identifying so closely with those I interview I am necessarily forfeiting any semblance of impartiality in my work.

But here is what I have discovered during these past few weeks, as I have toured the country reporting on what is often referred to as 'collateral damage', the human consequences of this terrible war both for Lebanon and the one and a half million Syrians who have sought refuge here, the many millions more scattered around the region and wandering dispossessed within their own country: I have discovered that there is no such thing as personal or public when it comes to displacement and suffering, no politics, no two sides to every story, no differing opinions and certainly no room for conjecture.

I have wondered why we allow ourselves to believe that refuge is a right for some while remaining a privilege for others. I have questioned how exactly we have come to accept that life and abundance are accidents of birth rather than a moral responsibility, how we reconcile this clear truth with the notion that the wretchedness of fellow human beings can reasonably be kept at arm's length, can be contained like this. The journalist in me ponders the lessons we might have learned but which we continue to ignore, the danger and shame in that ignorance, the inexorable storm that lies ahead.

I realize instead that as long as homelessness exists, I am — we all of us are — refugees. We are their fears and their frustration, their anguish and their undying will to survive, their optimism and their conviction that this world, somewhere, somehow, will always be their harbour.

Chapter 30

Arranging Fatima's escape to Turkey might prove to be her last accomplishment on the job, Maysoun muses. When she told Peter that the organization had helped refugees go through Syria to destinations further afield by allowing them to hide in ambulances, she had not been telling the whole truth. She had heard of one driver who, while transporting a wounded man from a battlefield to a hospital in Turkey, found a stowaway in the ambulance on arrival. The driver had not been disciplined because he had not known about it, but she realizes now that if it is discovered that she had helped Fatima and her children get away, her position as one of the top administrators of this organization might be compromised. Still, she has no intention of putting a stop to the plan; she senses everything that is defiant in her asserting itself.

Since Peter and Fatima came to see her, Maysoun

has determined which ambulance driver she will approach to take Fatima and her children to Turkey. When she meets with him, away from the office, she will reassure him that should he meet any trouble at any time during the trip or at its end, he is to say that she ordered him to allow Fatima and the children on to the ambulance and that he had had no choice but to follow that command. Once everything with the driver is arranged, all she will have to do is let Peter and Hannah know the date she has set for Fatima to depart.

She takes her reading glasses off, places them on her desk, lifts both arms above her head and stretches her upper body. She looks up when one of her colleagues appears at her office door.

—I'm going now, Maysoun, he says, looking and sounding as tired as she is. I guess you'll be the last one to leave so will you lock up?

—I'll be on my way too in a moment but yes, of course, I'll lock up. See you tomorrow.

But instead of preparing to leave, she finds that she is reluctant to move out of her chair. Is it because she feels some sense of an ending to what has been her life these past few years, to the path she seems at times inadvertently to have taken since she left Iraq?

She reaches for the laptop in her bag and places it on the desk once again. She searches for the Skype icon and telephones Jalal, though she cannot be sure he will be available at this hour.

Just as her call is answered and Jalal comes on to the screen, she realizes that since it is late afternoon in Beirut, it is very early in the morning in Auckland.

—Oh, no, she exclaims. I'm so sorry, I forgot what the time is there, Jalal. Please, go back to sleep. I'll hang up right away.

—No, no, don't go, he says. It is early here but I wasn't asleep. Look, I'm on my balcony having a coffee.

He turns the telephone around and she looks out on to what she imagines is the darkness of the South Pacific.

—I don't believe you, she laughs. I can't see anything at all.

—It's good to hear from you, Maysoun. His voice is softer now. How are things? Is Nazha still there with you?

—No, she left a few days ago. She's back in Baghdad. She refused to stay here.

She hears him sigh.

—Well, I understand why she would want to do that.

—Hmmm. Not sure I do, but tell me how are the girls? How are your sisters?

—They're all doing very well, *alhamdulillah*. They love it here, you know. He chuckles. I mean I had an idea the girls would like it when we came out here. But their aunts? I don't think they've ever enjoyed this much freedom. They have their own home not far from us and have made a good circle of friends among the community.

—But you like living there too, don't you? Maysoun asks.

—Yes, I do, but there are moments when I miss home. That's inevitable, isn't it?

—Of course it is. We all feel that way at some point, I suppose.

—Are you OK, Maysoun? You look a bit down. What's happened? How's your work going?

She sighs.

—I have to admit it's beginning to get to me. There's so much that needs to be put right and so little being done. Sometimes I feel the results we're achieving aren't worth all the effort. There are times when I just want to pick up and leave it all behind.

—I can understand how you must be feeling, he says. I believe the map of the Middle East is being deliberately redrawn through all this conflict. We were getting too close to liberating ourselves from dictators and corrupt governments a couple of years ago and the powers that be had to put a stop to that.

She shakes her head.

—I don't know, Jalal. I just think whatever the initial intentions behind the uprisings, things have spiralled out of control. There just doesn't seem to be any way out of all this. We're even having a difficult time trying to alleviate the suffering of refugees, whether in this part of the world or as they risk their lives trying to get to Europe.

—It's pointless worrying, especially when there's so little you can do about it anyway. I wish you would think seriously of leaving the region. There is a life out here, you know.

—Well, that's actually what I called to ask you about.

—Oh?

—I . . . I was just wondering if the invitation to come to New Zealand is still open. She gestures vaguely behind her. I mean I've only just realized that I need a break from all this, she continues.

He grins at her and she smiles back.

—I won't impose on you for long, she says.

He tells her that his hope is once she gets there that she will want to make of New Zealand a permanent home.

—That sounds perfect, Maysoun says, feeling something close to joy.

Chapter 31

At a tired café near the American University, Hannah
sits and looks outside where the weather is finally
turning, the sun less present and the air cooler, and
the torrential rains of a Beirut autumn, lightning and
its accompanying thunder, are anticipated. In the mountains, once temperatures drop, snow will also fall and,
for a short while at least, there will be the suggestion
of purity in a land no longer familiar with innocence.

Seeing Brigitte again had been unsettling, holding her
and whispering, 'I'm so sorry,' again and again, then
pulling away to look into her cool blue eyes and at her
pallor, at the impression of fading beauty and the intensity of a grief too private to penetrate. Had the children
been there, the pain and awkwardness of that first
encounter might have been avoided. As it was, she and
Peter, standing in the lobby of the small hotel their
friend was staying in, had watched as Brigitte attempted

to contain her emotions and felt something close to shame at not knowing what to say next in the way of comfort, waiting for her to invite them to sit down and ask them if they would like anything to drink so that they could refuse.

—I'm all right, Brigitte had eventually told them.

She paused before continuing.

—I'm here because I want Anas's exhibition to go ahead as planned. The children will join me soon, in time for the opening.

If Brigitte's words hinted at resilience, her demeanour, the way her hand trembled slightly as she lifted it to adjust a lock of hair, her unbending body, its stiffness, her manner of speech and the lack of shade in it, suggested otherwise. Hannah wondered if there was something she was not telling them; she looked more closely at her friend as she spoke and decided these were merely the markings of great sadness.

—I . . . I also need to put things right with Anas's family. His parents and sisters may be very angry with me right now but Rana and Marwan are all they have left of Anas and I don't want to keep the children away from them.

Hannah realized that what she had mistaken for woodenness in Brigitte's voice was, in fact, the result of nuances of German creeping back into her English, a kind of abruptness in speech that the many years spent in Syria immersed in Arabic had previously softened.

But she seemed to have been fortified by her sojourn home and that was exactly what she needed to face this ordeal.

As the evening wore on and turned into night, the small lobby dimly lit and quiet by then, as Hannah and Peter sat and Brigitte spoke, her voice rising then falling and lilting like waves, as they listened patiently to stories that needed to be told, of lives unravelling and the finality of death, it seemed to Hannah that a great emptiness stretched before them, sorrow gently beckoning, drawing them near.

Wondering where Brigitte's monologue would ultimately lead, Hannah leaned over in her seat and placed a hand on the other woman's arm in silent acknowledgement. She had been feeling so much guilt at Anas's death, both she and Peter had really, for allowing him to leave with Abou Mazen on his own, for returning to Beirut without him, for not reading the signs which with hindsight seemed a definite indication of Anas's real intentions. But if they had hoped for some kind of release in seeing and talking to his wife, in commiserating with her and expressing their own feelings, they did not find it.

If anything, Hannah now thinks, the regret at what could have been had they acted differently seems to have grown into something bigger, a weight that at times presses so hard into her chest that she discovers she has stopped breathing for a moment.

The café door opens and she looks up to see a group of students laden with backpacks and books. An older man, a professor perhaps, leads them to a table not far from hers. She glances at them surreptitiously at first and then more boldly as she follows their conversation, a class in history or politics or perhaps both, she is not sure. They discuss with their teacher the events of the past months and raise questions about possible outcomes and the disintegration of the region in the future. One young man raises his voice slightly to protest.

—As Arabs, he says, we are connected, there is a thread that stretches between us and cannot be broken.

Another disagrees.

—We are separate nations that undermine each other constantly and as a result we live incompletely.

For a moment, Hannah wishes her father were here with her. He is interested in the opinions of young people. Would he conclude, as she has, that youth does not make us immune from realizing the extent of our disgrace, but rather shames us into wondering what kind of legacy we are leaving behind?

By the time she leaves, rain has begun to fall. She hunches her shoulders, places her handbag over her head and runs, turning right on Hamra Street and then up Sadat Street and to her father's building where, drenched and shivering, she wipes her feet on the large mat in the entrance before getting into the lift and making her way upstairs. She shivers with cold as the housekeeper opens the door and lets her into the living room.

—Sweetheart, you got caught in the rain.

Faisal puts down his book and gets up from his armchair, frowning.

—Come with me, he says, leading her to a hall closet where he takes out a large towel and then pushes her gently towards the bathroom.

—I came to see you, *Baba*, Hannah says. So many things have happened and I haven't had the chance to talk to you about them.

—Yes, of course, *habibti*. We'll talk but first get out of those wet clothes and put on my robe. It's hanging behind the door. I'll turn the heater on in the living room so you can get yourself warm again.

There is something precious about elderly parents, Hannah tells herself, something that makes the inevitability of their loss seem more poignant still.

Chapter 32

—Is Hannah home? Brigitte asks, looking around in some confusion.

The young woman with an infant in her arms shakes her head.

—She's out, she says, looking closely at Brigitte. Are you the artist's wife? The one who was killed?

Brigitte gasps and the young woman motions to her to come inside.

—She told me to let you in if you got here before she did.

—Thank you.

—Are you from Syria? You sound like you're from home, but you don't look it. The woman reaches out to touch Brigitte's hair.

—No, no. I'm not Syrian but my husband is.

Brigitte makes her way to the sitting room and sees a young boy playing on the carpet by the French doors.

He looks up at her and smiles. He is very much like his mother, has light-coloured eyes and fair skin. The baby begins to cry and the mother places it on the sofa before going into the kitchen. It looks to be about three months old and, unlike the little boy, has a full head of dark, wavy hair.

—A little girl? Brigitte asks when she comes back with a bottle.

The young woman nods.

Leaving the baby on the sofa, she pushes the bottle into her mouth and holds it there, turning her head away to stare at Brigitte.

Having lived in the Middle East for so long, she is used to standing out because of her height and her blonde hair, but she has a feeling that the young woman's apparent fascination with her has something else behind it.

—I'm from Syria, the young woman says.

—Oh.

Brigitte cannot understand why she feels uncomfortable in this woman's presence.

—My husband was killed in the war too, she continues. I didn't want to leave our home but I had to in the end.

—I'm sorry, Brigitte manages to say after a pause.

The young woman clears her throat.

—He was looking for you, your husband. I heard him talk to the others about it, about how anxious he was that you took the children away.

Brigitte lifts her head in astonishment.

—You were here? You met Anas?

She nods.

—My son and I were staying here too.

—I don't understand.

The young woman looks confused.

—I'm Fatima. Hannah hasn't told you about me?

Brigitte shakes her head.

—I only just got here, she says. I was in Germany . . .

—Yes, he told me that you'd taken the children away with you.

—Anas?

—He went out on to the balcony to smoke a cigarette and I followed him. We talked for a long time.

—You talked to him about us? Brigitte asks softly.

—When he explained what had happened, what you had done, I told him he was wrong, that there wasn't a mother in the world who wouldn't want to get her children out of that place, that he had no right to expect anything different from you.

Brigitte cannot believe what she is hearing.

—Anyway, Fatima continues, he didn't say very much at first. But I could tell he was listening. Then just before we went back inside, he showed me a picture of you and the children, your son and daughter.

Brigitte opens her eyes wide in astonishment.

—I told him that if he was missing you all, he should

just go to you. I said that's what I intended to do, go be with my family no matter what. Eventually, he agreed with me, said he knew he couldn't live without you and the children.

—He mentioned me?

—Yes.

Brigitte takes a deep breath and, feeling suddenly cold, wraps her arms around herself.

—Can I hold her? she finally asks.

Fatima nods and hands her the baby.

She nestles the infant in the crook of her arm and watches as she sucks eagerly at the bottle. Her forehead is high, delicate skin stretched thinly over it, revealing tiny, crisscross veins of colour. Brigitte bends down to take in that inimitable scent of baby, of newness, and is instantly refreshed.

Recollections of her own children as infants flood into her mind, pictures such as this, of Anas standing patiently beside her, looking on with tenderness and then taking the bundle on to his shoulder to relieve her for a few moments, listening to him sing the babies to sleep, watching him rock them in his arms; memories of his immense, unrelenting love for them. Her tears fall on to the child's blanket and she is unable to stop them. She looks around for a tissue and is grateful when Fatima hands her one.

—He was a good man, your husband, Fatima says suddenly. He was kind to me.

Brigitte nods, her head still down, unable to speak.

—When I said your husband was a kind man, I meant I knew he'd be able to help me.

A look of anxiety passes over her face and Brigitte is suddenly aware, as one sometimes is, that she is about to be taken into Fatima's confidence.

—Before they took me back to the camp in the south, she says, he promised to help me.

—What camp?

—When my son and I fled Damascus and came to this country, we joined members of my husband's family in an encampment in the south.

—But how did you come to be here, in Beirut?

—I left her here. Fatima points to the baby. I've had to come back for her because the woman looking after her no longer wants her.

Brigitte does not know what any of this has to do with Anas.

—I told him about the baby, you see, Fatima continues. She was born long after my husband died. He understood why I couldn't keep her.

—You're not keeping her?

—You'll need to burp her now, Fatima says, ignoring the comment.

Brigitte lifts the baby on to her shoulder and pats her gently on the back.

—You think I'm heartless, I know, Fatima says.

—No. I—

—But I have to think of my son. I have to think about his future. There's no place for a sister with no name in it.

The baby lets out a soft burp and Brigitte smiles despite herself.

—But I don't understand how Anas was able to help you, she says, and in that moment, looking at the young mother, the child's breathing aligned with her own, Brigitte understands. He told you he would find a home for her, didn't he? she asks quietly.

The young woman continues to look at her, saying nothing.

—He didn't suggest we would take her, did he?

When Fatima nods in reply, Brigitte feels shaken and is not sure whether or not to believe her. Maybe Anas didn't have a chance to tell me about it, Brigitte thinks. Peter had said that, just before leaving, Anas told him he had finally understood why she had decided to leave with the children. But when he had gone on to Damascus despite that, Brigitte concluded that he might have changed his mind. Oh, God, she wonders, what had Anas really been thinking when he told this woman he would be prepared to take her baby?

She looks down at the child in her arms again, the wide-open eyes and that stillness in them that one sees only in infants, a kind of quiet knowing, and for an instant it is as though Anas is standing beside her, also looking on in wonder.

—*Habibi*, Brigitte whispers to herself, dare I believe that you died loving me still?

She is aware moments later of the little boy standing up and going over to his mother. Fatima takes him on to her lap and kisses the top of his head.

—This is Wassim, she says.

—Hello, Wassim.

The baby begins to hiccup and Wassim screws up his face.

Brigitte looks at him.

—What's the baby's name? she asks him.

He turns his head to look at his mother but Fatima only shrugs.

The baby begins to squirm in Brigitte's arms.

—I think she needs changing, she says. Would you like me to do it?

Fatima lifts the little boy off her lap and puts him back on to the floor.

—Go get the nappies from the kitchen, she tells him. The ones Hannah bought for us. Then she places a rectangle of cloth on the carpet and turns to Brigitte. You can lie her down here, she says.

But Brigitte is unwilling to let her off so easily.

—What is the baby's name? she asks again.

Fatima sighs.

—She doesn't have one.

—Doesn't have a name? she asks with disbelief. Why not?

Wassim comes in with the bag of nappies and Fatima hands her one, a look of resignation passing across her face.

—If I give her a name, I'll have to keep her.

—But she's your child . . .

—Mine? What use do I have for a girl? She'll just be another burden for me – and for Wassim as well, eventually. And once she gets older, what chance will she have without a father to protect her?

—You cannot abandon your child, Brigitte says as she changes the baby. Surely you realize that much?

Fatima stands up.

—I'm not abandoning her, am I? she says, her voice rising. You're all good people here. You can take care of her. And why do you keep saying she's mine? I never said she was, did I?

—I'm sorry. I don't mean to upset you . . .

Fatima sits down again and begins to sob.

—You know, when I heard about your husband being killed, she finally says, looking up at Brigitte, the first thing I thought of was how difficult it would be for you, like it was for me. She shakes her head. I mean I know you're much better off and everything, but the feelings are the same. I cared about my husband too and he loved me back in his own way, just like yours did. I could tell he did, the way he talked about you and everything. It wasn't just about the children for him.

Before Brigitte can reply, the front door opens and
Peter and Hannah walk in.

—Oh, you're here already. Hannah comes up and
gives her a hug. Squeezed between them, the baby lets
out a little yelp. Hannah laughs.

—So you've met Fatima and the children, she says.

—Peter kisses Brigitte.

—Sorry we're late. We were held up at Maysoun's.

—Fatima, Hannah says. We have good news. It's all
arranged for the day after tomorrow, for you and the
children.

The young woman looks anxious.

—Don't worry, *habibti*, Hannah says. Brigitte is a
close friend. She won't say anything.

—I'll go in and start supper, Peter says.

He turns to Fatima and Wassim.

—You two can come and help me, he says with a
smile, and they follow him into the kitchen.

Brigitte looks at Hannah.

—She met with Anas when he was here, spoke to
him . . .

—Yes, I know. He was the only one of us she would
talk to in the beginning.

—Would you believe I'm feeling jealous? she says,
close to tears. About their conversation, I mean. It's
much more than he gave me in the end.

—Come here, Hannah says gently, taking her friend
into her arms.

Perhaps what I need to do, Brigitte tells herself, is to grieve without hope of comfort and without aim, with no view to the future, no expectation of resolution, to wallow in the guilt of my own survival and imagine, uselessly, frenziedly, what might have been. She wants to smile at these thoughts but feels herself cave in instead, her chest and all her insides turning in on themselves so that she is reduced to one, beating centre.

*

On the balcony with Hannah and Peter, Brigitte feels a chill in the air. It is late enough for the streets to be relatively empty of traffic but many of the windows in the buildings across from them, beyond the now dark courtyard and on a level with the unseen sea, still flicker with light.

—She has no intention of taking the baby with her, Brigitte says, her voice a little too loud. I hope you two realize that.

—What do you mean? asks Peter.

—I mean exactly that. Fatima is planning to leave the baby here.

—How do you know that? Hannah asks.

Brigitte shifts in her seat.

—I had a chance to talk to her before you arrived earlier this evening and she told me that's what she was going to do. She says she spoke to Anas before he left for Damascus and he promised to visit the baby at the Palestinian camp and help her arrange for someone to take it.

—But he never mentioned anything about that to us, Hannah protests, leaning forward in her seat.

—She probably made him promise not to, Peter says. She was much more comfortable talking to him than she was with us.

—But I still don't believe she would abandon her baby if no one agreed to take it.

—I think she's desperate enough to do it, Brigitte continues. She is absolutely adamant that she cannot take that child with her to join her family.

Peter frowns and reaches out to touch his wife's arm.

—I think Brigitte's right, Hannah, he says. We need to sort this out.

—But what can we do? Just hand her over to the authorities here and forget about the whole thing?

They fall silent for a few moments, mulling over their thoughts in the dark.

—I want her, Brigitte blurts out. I'll take her.

—I'm sorry?

—If Anas promised he would help her, then it's my responsibility now to do that. She also told me he told her he would be prepared to take the baby himself.

—And you believed her?

—It doesn't matter if I believe her or not, Brigitte

says emphatically. The important thing is that this child needs to be saved from an uncertain fate.

Hannah and Peter remain silent.

—Why are you looking at me like that? she asks.

—Do you realize what you're saying, Brigitte? Hannah finally asks.

—Of course I do.

—You've had a big shock, *habibti*. This may not be the best time to make such a big decision.

Brigitte shakes her head.

—I didn't have to think about leaving Damascus when I did, she says.

—But will you take her back to Berlin with you?

Brigitte shakes her head.

—I'm not sure we're going back there.

—What? You're not planning to go back to Damascus, are you?

—No, of course not. But the children and I love it here. So did Anas. We could stay on in Beirut. Look, it may seem crazy to you, Hannah, but I know in my heart it's the right thing to do. Please don't look so shocked. I've already spoken to my in-laws about this and they're very happy we'll be close by. This is where we belong, Hannah – or where my children and I can at least learn to belong.

—All I'm saying is that you should give yourself more time to think about it. Don't let it be an impulse decision like this.

Brigitte presses her lips together.

—How can I explain? she asks quietly. To you, my kind and loving friends. But something is compelling me to do this, some instinct . . .

—Do you know what has just occurred to me? Peter suddenly intervenes. And then, without waiting for an answer, he continues: I've just realized that this is exactly the kind of thing Anas would do – you know, resolving to save this child – absolutely the kind of decision he would have made, given the circumstances. I'm sure of it.

He looks at Brigitte and smiles.

—It's almost as if, he tells her, it's almost as if in taking this child you will be making up in some way for the loss of Anas. This is what 'a life for a life' really means.

Brigitte's heart, which had begun to drop moments earlier, suddenly lifts and floats towards him. He has given her the answer she needed. She feels that Anas himself has spoken to her through Peter, as if he made the decision long before she could have been aware of it and all she needs to do now is receive it with grace. She mouths a silent thank you to Peter, sits back in her chair and closes her eyes to the Beirut night.

Chapter 33

It is raining hard, though it is not cold. Hannah waits for Peter to come around to her with the umbrella and steps out of the car. Standing now, she can see the open doorway of the gallery and the people inside, bright lights and fluid movement, shelter from the deluge.

She holds on to her husband's arm and they walk slowly beneath the umbrella, looking down to try and avoid the puddles that are appearing in ever-expanding circles at their feet. Peter is tall and sturdily built. She leans against him as if she might benefit from his height, from the larger space he occupies in this world, and in becoming aware of their bodies, close and cautious as they move together like this, she realizes how much she has depended on him during this past and difficult year, wonders how she would have coped, given the turmoil around them, without this man who now walks in step with her with such ease.

The exhibition has attracted more people than she could have imagined and it is difficult to move around once they get inside. She lets go of Peter's arm and moments later when she looks behind her he is no longer there. Unable to see Brigitte and the children, Hannah decides to peruse the paintings and sculptures that had been scattered haphazardly around the gallery when she came here with Anas weeks ago and which are now beautifully displayed. As she does so, despite all the activity around her, she can sense Anas's presence, his critical artist's eye.

From him, she had learned to see works of art from a new perspective: how to look beyond the obvious and assess an object's relationship with its surroundings; how colour and light are one and the same; how the observer and the thing being observed continually shape one another; and, perhaps most importantly, that beauty is not merely a reflection of taste but is, on some level, an absolute. It seems to her, looking at these works of art that keep safe so much of what was precious about Anas, that art is also a purveyor of truth. If his violent death is a symbol of the betrayal of the popular revolts that brought down merciless regimes all over the Arab world, then Anas's art is the antithesis of that treachery, an indication that life will always find ways to assert itself, no matter the circumstances. She feels sudden anguish that had he lived, Anas would surely have achieved still greater recognition for his work, and that with his loss, the region had lost not only an artist but a man whose awareness and insight had brought grace and clarity to an otherwise dim and despondent environment.

She spots Brigitte in the far corner of the gallery and makes her way over to her. Marwan and Rana, dressed in their best clothes, are standing beside their mother and baby Hayat sleeps in a pram next to them. Brigitte is busy greeting well-wishers so Hannah bends down to talk to the children.

—Everything OK here? she asks cheerfully.

—Shhh. Rana places a finger over her mouth. You'll wake the baby, Aunty Hannah.

—I'm sorry, sweetheart, Hannah says quietly. I didn't mean to do that. Amazing that she can go on sleeping with all the noise around her, isn't it?

—I'm not letting anyone come near her, that's why, Rana replies. You'd better move away too now.

—Yes, yes, of course I will.

Hannah takes Marwan by the hand.

—Will you show me around, *habibi*? Since you know your father's work so well, you'll be the best guide.

Although he does not say anything, Marwan follows her to where one of Hannah's favourites, a clay sculpture, is displayed on a column that has been painted in white. The setting makes the figure appear even smaller than it actually is, its head round and disproportionately large, its diminutive arms sprouting from either side of its torso, its eyes hollow indentations that appear to have been pressed – as one would press fingers into dough – on to the front of its skull.

—What do you think of this one? she asks Marwan.

He drops her hand and does not look at her. In the days since his arrival, he has maintained a pretence of nonchalance, of feigned indifference, that has alarmed Hannah. When she expressed her concern, Peter told her that Marwan might simply not be ready to face his grief. 'Give him time, Hannah. Give them all time to come to terms with what's happened.'

—I think, Hannah says now, this is a fun piece, kind of quirky. Just like your dad was. Know what I mean?

Marwan lifts his hands up towards her, and gives her the thumbs up. She raises her eyebrows and waits for what will come next.

—Who do you think made those eyes look like that? he asks her.

When she finally understands, she laughs out loud, grabs his thumbs with her hands and shakes them hard.

—Ah, it was you, she says, and is delighted when Marwan grins back at her. That's why it's so good. No wonder I loved it so much when I first saw it. Then, more quietly, she asks: You really liked working with your father, didn't you?

Marwan nods.

—He took me to his studio lots of times, he says. He always wanted to know what I thought of what he was working on and let me work with him on some stuff too. I mean, I don't know if I would ever want to be an artist like he is but it was fun to play around with paint and clay. I don't know, maybe I should become an artist now and sell my work too.

—You know, Marwan, Hannah says gently, he always told me how proud he was of you, said he wanted you to do whatever would make you happy.

The boy looks at her anxiously.

—But now that he's dead, it's up to me to take care of everyone – my mother and my sister . . . my sisters, I mean. Somebody has to earn a living to keep this family going.

Hannah tries not to smile.

—You're right, *habibi*, but you know your mother is very strong and very capable. I've always admired her for that. She'll take care of things, I'm certain of that. Besides, Uncle Peter and I will always be here for you if you need us.

As if on cue, Peter appears.

—Hello, he says. Marwan, where have you been? I've been looking for you. He gestures to the young boy to follow him. Come with me. There's a young man who wants to meet you, the son of a great friend of your father's. Let's grab some juice and take it over to him.

—And this is why I love you, Hannah whispers into the air as she watches them walk away.

275

A waiter with a tray of tiny canapés comes by. She grabs a few and is munching on them when Maysoun, dressed in a long green dress that brings out the colour of her eyes and makes her skin glow, comes up to her.

—I don't think I've ever seen you looking so beautiful, Hannah tells her friend as they embrace. Something wonderful must be happening in your life.

—I do have some news. I'm leaving at the end of the month. Finally going to New Zealand.

—To see that friend you told me about? I know you've spoken about it before but I didn't think it would be so soon.

Hannah finishes the last morsel of food, wipes her mouth with a napkin and looks for somewhere to throw it out.

—If I like it there, continues Maysoun, he says he wants me to stay on.

—You mean you'll get married?

—I'm not sure about that but it's a possibility, I guess.

—Will your mother go with you?

—She's refusing to so far, but she might be persuaded if I decide to stay.

Hannah wonders if Maysoun isn't just running away and will later regret her decision to go to the other side of the world in search of happiness.

—Are you pleased to be leaving, *habibti*? she dares to ask. Is it what you really want?

Maysoun pauses for a moment before replying.

—I know what I don't want, she says. I don't want to be alone and I don't want to be working in a job and in a part of the world where despair is always the order of the day. Does that sound terribly selfish to you?

—No, of course it doesn't. You deserve to be happy, Maysoun.

Hannah reaches out and gives her friend another hug.

—I don't think I've thanked you enough for what you did for Fatima and her son. We were thrilled to hear that they're settling in well at the camp in Turkey.

Maysoun smiles.

—Yes, I was very glad about that too, but what about the baby?

—You mean Hayat? She's over there.

Hannah points to the pram that Rana is now pushing towards the Ladies with Brigitte following closely behind.

—It's wonderful, isn't it? Sometimes things do come full circle, despite the odds. Brigitte had decided to name the baby Hayat, meaning life, and they had all agreed that it was both beautiful and appropriate.

Maysoun plants a kiss on Hannah's cheek.

—Let's spend as much time as we can together before I leave for New Zealand. Maysoun turns and walks away as if floating on a cloud.

If we each take different paths in our lives, Hannah wonders, then how true can my interpretation of someone else's journey be? Maysoun will leave and I will miss her at first, will try and recall how her story once touched my own until eventually even that memory of memories past will fade.

She looks around for Peter and finds him by the statuette she had been looking at with Marwan earlier.

—You like this one too, she says, slipping her hand into his.

He turns around and smiles.

—Something about it is very appealing, isn't it? It reminds me so much of Anas.

She leans her head against his shoulder.

—You know, Hannah says wistfully, there was something I always wanted to ask him but I never got the chance.

—Hmmm?

—I wanted to ask how exactly he knew when whatever he was working on was finished? How do you know when it is time to stop painting or sculpting or writing or composing something?

—When it's complete, you mean?

She nods.

—Well, Peter continues, Anas and I talked about something like that once. He told me he always felt he had to attempt not just to create perfection as a final goal but to continue to recreate it again and again as he worked, with every brushstroke of paint, every groove in clay. Maybe what he was trying to say is that there is neither beginning nor end to any kind of endeavour. That it's the creative process that is its own reward.

278

Hannah looks at him, marvels at how familiar his face has become to her, and how great is the comfort, how tender the emotion, at times like these of mutual recognition. How had she ever doubted his love for her or hers for him?

—We're both tired, Peter says with a smile. All this talk about life and art is a bit much, isn't it?

She laughs.

—Shall we go? he asks.

When we get to the exit, I turn around to take one last look, note the light and sound, the movement and moments of stillness in between. I see in this scene the completeness that Anas had sought in his work and life, the beauty that is displayed here and the people who seek and are moved by it. Most of all, I understand that there is a purpose to all this, that Anas's death has in part been vindicated, and that suffering does not endure as long as the will is there to let it go.

—Peter?

He looks at her but she's not sure what it is she wants to say so she reaches out and places a hand on his arm instead.

—How about we pay a visit to your father before we go home? he asks. It would be nice to be with him right now, don't you think?

—Yes, *habibi*. Yes, it would.

Once in the car, and despite the rain, Hannah opens her window just a little and breathes in the humid air. Peter has taken the coastal road, driving first through the downtown area, rebuilt since the war but still lacking the soul and vibrancy of the old Beirut, and then onto the Corniche where the blue-black sea menaces, waves rising high over a barrier of rocks on the shoreline before splashing onto the road and the vehicles moving cautiously across it.

She remembers her conversation with Anas as they walked here weeks ago, her assertion that she could only ever be really happy living by this sea and his argument, in turn, that Peter might have sacrificed a great deal because of that.

For a moment, she begins to ask herself if she would have been prepared to do the same for Peter, leave family and home behind just to be with him, then recalls the many times he has insisted that his wish was only that they be together, wherever that might be.

She looks out at her Beirut once again, at night and oblivion advancing and feels, inexplicably, a quiet gratitude. And when Peter, as if recognizing a need in her, reaches out to touch her lightly on the shoulder, she turns to him, his profile indistinct now, imbued with the darkness that surrounds them, takes his hand and lifts it to her cheek.